Hunters

Hunters

UNNI M. KAKANADAN

PARTRIDGE

A Penguin Random House Company

To order additional copies of this book, contact
Partridge India
000 800 10062 62
orders.india@partridgepublishing.com

www.partridgepublishing.com/india

To my uncle Ajoy Ignatius, who taught me how to club the letters for the very first time in my life, to my sister, Roshni Roges, and to my brother, Ullas Kakanadan, and to all others in this universe.

Acknowledgment

$\mathcal{I}$ would like to thank my Partridge Publishing associates, James Clifford and Gemma Ramos, for assisting me in getting this book published. I would like to thank my parents, Mohan and Moncy; my close ones—Rafi J. Louis, Joshna Thomas, Benjy Mathew, Anju Varghese, Shruthi Shyam, Varsha Dinesh—for their sincere support in one way or another and their pleasant casual talks from around the globe. Last but not the least, to my all-time Lady Luck and to the doctors and nurses of Ernakulum Medical Centre who treated me after a major accident a few years back. Had it not been for them, you won't be reading my book now.

Contents

Prologue

*I*n a dark forbidden land, three humans wearing black latex suits with a reddish *Hs* insignia on their chests were combating with their swords against two dragons. One dragon was in a reddish humanoid form wearing a green cloth around its waist, and the other in a reddish humanoid form wearing a yellow cloth around its waist. They were muscular, and each stood about eight feet tall.

"Dragoon! You can't betray our friendships or the lives we swore to protect," said a lady with long blackish-brown hair, brandishing her sword.

"Right, we shouldn't have, but we have no other choice," said the reddish-yellow humanoid dragon, "if you lot won't cooperate."

"Power is taking over your heads," said a blond young man.

"Nothing's taking over our heads," said the other humanoid.

"No, Shenron, it is. Why don't you guys understand?" said a black-haired young man. "We're breaking apart. We can't go into what we're against. We're the forces of good against evil."

"What did we get?" said the reddish-green humanoid.

"Shenron," said the gal, "we have learned never to ask anything in return for a good deed from our hearts."

"Hell with the lessons," said Shenron. "We had too much. Now better stop aiming for heaven."

"Yeah!" said Dragoon.

Shenron stamped the ground with force, jumped, and transformed into a vicious dragon, and so did Dragoon. Both breathed fierce fire at the trio below. The trio jumped into the dark waters beside them.

The dragons flew off, and the trio resurfaced and walked onto the bank. The black-haired man and the blackish-brown-haired lady sat on a dead log on the bank as the blond man rested his back on a large rock opposite the log.

The black-haired man said, "Everything's falling apart in the friendship between the five of us."

Both men looked at her, and all three looked with sorrow at the far-flying dragons, which were now fading dots.

The girl said sadly, "Yeah."

Later, far away, the two dragons sat on two rocks in a big cave, facing each other in their near humanoid forms.

Shenron said, "I believe the five of us have split now."

Dragoon said, "Yeah, now those three humans are in one group, and we two dragons are in another."

Shenron said, "Flireon was right, humans will go against us."

"Flireon is gone," said Dragoon, "and won't be back till we both lose our lives."

Shenron said, "Yeah, that's never gonna happen, and good thing we dealt with Flireon before the rift began."

"Yeah," said Dragoon, "those three humans really gave that Flireon a heck of a headache. Ha ha ha."

Shenron laughed too.

"But first, let us begin terrorizing here, and then we'll exploit one world after another," said Dragoon, and he laughed.

Shenron said, smiling wickedly, "Yeah."

One

he universe is vast, and it has many secrets. There are many universes. They are also called realms. This is Realm 115 out of the 126 realms or universes scattered, and in here, this particular story, Hunters, unfolds as you read. On the Earth in Realm 115, humans live, sharing the world with many supernatural forces, like wizards, fairies, witches, gremlins, goblins, and monsters. There were constant battles and wars between all the races. Even the human race got involved. And when other races began threatening innocent human lives, a secret society known as the Hunters rose to fight such evil forces.

One night in the Hunters' secret lair in an underground sewer, an elderly Chinese man with thick white hair and a beard and wearing a red Hawaiian shirt and black trousers was working, drawing some circles with alphabets and numbers from zero to nine on a sheet of paper and rolling two large rectangular red dice.

He stared at the fan revolving overhead and said to himself, "Marco, you are next."

"Marco? Who's Marco, Mr. Ching?" said a blond-haired, well-built man who was playing cards with a beautiful lady with long blackish-brown hair and a black-haired black man.

"I just calculated it, Alex," said Ching. "The new Hunter is Marco, one of my students. I knew he is destined to be one of us, but I never thought his time is at hand."

"What do you mean, and how do your circles, dice, and numbers work in finding out the next newcomer?" said the long-haired brunette.

"One and two, he's a student in my school, and haven't I told you about the real founders? He's one of the true founders. And three, mathematics, kiddo, mathematics," said Ching.

"I hate mathematics," said the lady.

"Now that I can't help unless you say where you got the difficulties," said Ching.

"Yeah, as if am not trying," said the lady with a disappointed face.

"Oh, poor lass," said the blond-haired man, laughing.

"So are you gonna tell him now? And what about the other two?" asked the lady, not bothered by his teasing.

"Wait . . . I'll tell when it's time, and as for the other two, they too will soon enter, and their time might be soon as one is already back," said Ching, looking at the sewage flowing ahead.

On a fine day almost a week later, after the classes in Merriam University (MU) in New York were left off at noon after calling it a day, Marco, a teen of seventeen with dark-green eyes and black curtained hair, decided to visit the house of one of his favorite science professors, Prof. Ching, and check on his well-being as he had not been well for the past four to five days and was on leave. Marco reached the house, stood near the door, and rang the calling bell.

First, a single rough and loud *ting tong* sounded loudly from the bell and then a soft chirping of a bird.

After a few minutes, an elderly man with blue eyes and thick white beard and hair and wearing a loose red shirt and white-striped black pajamas opened the door and, seeing Marco, said, "Oh, come in, Marco."

"Hope I'm not disturbing you, Mr. Ching!" said Marco.

"Oh no, no, no, my dear boy, I was just going through some of my books and had dozed off, so I didn't notice the time flying by. Good thing you came and woke me up," said Ching, laughing, "as I don't usually take these noon naps. Today I just dozed off while sitting bored."

Marco smiled too and said, "Oh."

"Good thing you came . . . I had wanted to meet you for the past few days," said Ching.

"Yeah, what is it, sir?" said Marco.

Ching asked Marco to follow him into a large room which was dark except for the light coming from a candle placed far on the table on the other end of the room. Marco noticed that the room was dark and was empty except for a bookshelf with a few books, a mat kept rolled and slanting to it, and a sword on the wall.

Ching took the mat, unrolled it, and laid it on the floor, asking Marco to be seated. Mr. Ching just stood, and he began, "I don't know how much you like supernatural phenomena—"

"I love it, in fact, and that too, vastly," interrupted Marco.

"That's good," said Ching as he sat on the other end of the mat opposite to Marco. "As in our kind of slayers of evil, or Hunters, a fact—"

"You're a hunter? Wow . . ." said Marco, again interrupting.

3

"Hmm . . . I knew you would join us. I recently came to know," said Ching, "that a new Hunter is gonna come and that it's a boy. You. Well, that was uncalculated. You're born to be a Hunter to fight such evils and to strengthen this legacy of the Hunters."

Marco was shocked.

"I myself," Ching said, signaling Marco to be silent by placing a finger on his own lips, "am a Hunter, a supernatural hunter . . . one among many others. I found it out through some spells just a week before that you're destined to be a new Hunter. The sword identical to the one on the wall is your weapon against them, and I will give you a potion. You have to apply it on the sword anyhow. And then open the book, and the enemy will be captured in it forever. You have to create a destructive ring, which you will learn in the meantime from the notes I have prepared for you, and I'll demonstrate it to you. And then put the potion on the book, and all the captured ones will be released from the book and into that destructive energy ring that you have created, and they'll meet their doom. None can escape from it as the ring will pull them into it like a vacuum pump pulls the dust off a sofa, and thus you can reuse the book and continue protecting the world."

"But then, why the sword?" asked Marco.

"A cut is necessary to capture them so that the liquid touches their blood when you splash it on them after you cut them," replied Ching.

"The applying and capturing are just to make the fight short for a time being," said Ching, "unless you decide to kill them with your sword fast. If the page with their sketch gets torn off, then they can again be free to wreak havoc on the innocents."

Marco heard all this and was shocked, open-mouthed, and then Ching got up and went toward the shelf and took a sword from its second layer and brought it along with a book and a potion in a flask and a few sheets of paper clipped together.

He placed the clipped sheets of paper, book, and potion down and then removed the sword from the sheath. He raised the sword and waved it to the left and then to the right and then above, then an orangish-reddish-yellow circle was created. And then he said, "This is how the destructive circle is made." Holding the sword with his left hand, he swiped the air to the left side, still holding it with one hand, and the circle vanished.

Marco sat open-mouthed and amazed at what he just saw. Ching then handed the sword to Marco. Marco got up and took it, extending both his hands forward, and then he bowed to Ching. Ching told Marco to do as he just showed, and Marco did it correctly on the fifth try. Concentration was heavily required. Ching handed over the rest of the items and sat down. Marco sat too.

"These swords were dipped into that potion once when they were made so they can hurt any supernatural, and you can apply a bit of the potion again so that the potion will get stuck on the sword and the enemy can be easily captured instead of a longer fight and more destructions. And the book too was dipped once when it was created, so there is no need to dip it again, and it can help in capturing one," said Ching. "And your Hunter suit is in the making. You will have it soon. Till then, cover your identity in any way possible. Any doubts, you can ask."

Marco didn't know what to ask or say as he was still in a kind of shock, and so he shook his head.

"Well, you go home and study then," said Ching.

Marco nodded and left.

Marco took a quick glance by shuffling a few pages. The book was old but empty and filled with blank pages, and the flask contained a strange reddish-blue liquid. Two pages were stuck together, but he didn't notice it while shuffling the pages fast. The sword was magnificent and long. It looked similar to the one on the wall. Its handle was brownish, and the sword was broader toward the edge. He took a look at the notes Ching had prepared for him about the destructive ring's creation and a few tips.

Marco was thrilled and amazed and was excited to tell all this to his best friend, Matt, later. That day, with excitement, Marco sent a message to Matt, asking him to come to his place that night to stay over. Some milliseconds had passed when Matt's reply came, agreeing with a smiley and a thumbs-up emoji.

In a chemical base somewhere in town, things began to go wrong, and by evening, they did go wrong. The container holding a nuclear liquid was developing cracks, and by evening, it cracked open and all the liquid poured out. As it had closed early that day, no workers were there to notice the leak until the next day.

Meantime, a firefly looking for a way out got an electric shock after sitting on a wire, and it fell down into the flowing nuclear liquid below and drowned with minute sparks of life in it.

That night, Matt, a blond, chubby fellow, came over for a sleepover. Marco told him everything.

"Wow . . . it's ridiculous and strange," said Matt.

Marco said, "Yeah, I know, and I too feel the same way, but you know Mr. Ching isn't mostly the one who makes jokes in the class like the others, and so hearing all this Hunter thing coming from his mouth gives me creeps."

"Hmm . . ." said Matt. "That I too will agree with."

The night passed normally. Matt was thrilled that Marco became a Hunter, who hunted down supernatural beings, and Matt would be his partner coz there was no way he was gonna let his best childhood pal have all the fun and thrill while he sits and studies, preparing for the boring class the next day.

The next morning at the nuclear chemical base staring at the big puddle of the toxic water,. "Find the leak and mend it," ordered a fat, brown-haired man wearing an orange helmet, who looked like the leader.

As the leak was found and the mending was going on at the place where the liquid had accumulated in large quantities, the liquid rose, and out flew a gigantic firefly. It had mutated in features too as it now had a blinking sting at the end of its tail instead of just a blinking light. It killed about seven people when it attacked with the sting it had grown at the tip of its tail. The base was shut down, and everyone ran out. Moreover, the insect caused a power failure within the chemical base when it destroyed the powerhouse.

It was soon all over the news as the creature flew out into the city and started creating havoc. Matt and Marco, who were returning from their college, also saw it on TV in a store where everyone was glued to the news. Both looked at each other, and Marco gave a wicked smile.

Matt knew the glint in his pal's eyes and said, "Don't think of it."

He told Matt to follow him and rode to the city. Matt followed, shouting, "But you don't have the items, do you?"

Marco said, "Yup, I have them in my bag. Can't say when they'll come in handy, like now."

Matt said, "But the news said it seems to be a genetically mutated firefly, so it's not a supernatural phenomenon."

"But also we don't get to see a firefly so monstrous every day. So it's supernatural no matter how it's here," said Marco to Matt. "You go back to your home."

"While you alone have the fun?" said Matt. "No way, dude. I'm coming with you if you're going."

After ten minutes of argument on whether Matt would go home or not, finally, still racing to the city, it was decided at last that Matt would come. Marco sped up his cycle through the blocks with Matt following him closely behind. After an hour, they reached the city. Many buildings were destroyed, and many were evacuating. At that time, they saw a Hunter fighting the monster. The Hunter saw them and came toward them, jumping and avoiding stings, debris, and attacks. He approached them and removed the cloth which hid his face, so that they could know who he was exactly. It was Ching!

Matt thought Ching would tell Marco to back out as this was not a case for an amateur to handle.

"Thanks you are here," said Ching, wearing his mask back on to Matt's horror. "It's creating havoc in the city. I could use your help as I am bit too old now. But cover your faces with some cloth for now. You don't need anyone tracking your moves later."

Marco smiled and said, "Yes, sir," and they rode a few paces ahead as Ching indicated with his hand.

Marco and Matt took out their towels from their pockets and tied them around their heads, hiding their faces except for their eyes.

Marco looked at Matt. Matt kept quiet, disbelieving that Ching didn't turn them away.

As three hours passed by, Ching borrowed Marco's sword after losing his sword into a big crack on the road and threatened the monster by throwing strong cyclonic winds by stroking some moves in the air. It fought with its sting as Ching used the sword. He even created a storm using the sword and had the firefly crash into a skyscraper.

The boys were amazed. Marco even noted Ching's style in creating the cyclonic blast. The beast flew and started attacking Ching again. Ching defended himself but was a bit weak from the fight as he was old.

The boys noticed it, but they didn't know how they could help more as there was only one sword, and that too was with Ching as he had lost the other one into a crack. Ching asked Marco to throw the flask to him, and Marco took it from his bag and threw it to him. Marco and Matt watched what Ching was gonna do now.

They watched as Ching applied some liquid on the sword with his fingers and attacked. After two to three tries, he had the liquid touch the sting. He told Marco to throw him the book, and Marco did. As Ching was defending himself, he lost his balance and fell on an iron rod among the broken debris. To the boys' horror, the rod penetrated through Ching. Still Ching got up and opened the book, and there was a huge wind as the firefly was sucked into it. The boys ran to Ching, who was bleeding profusely.

Ching looked at Marco and said, "It's over at last, and so is my time, it seems."

Marco asked, "Why didn't you use the liquid or book before?"

"I was in town since yesterday, visiting a friend, and didn't take them. I thought, what was gonna happen if I didn't take it for a day? And not even the mask or costume. Sword I got as I had brought it. Didn't feel like coming out totally open for attacks. It was the wrong decision," said Ching. "You two keep this a secret and go, and I had called for my friends . . . They'll be here, and then you go and maintain our secret."

The boys cried silently with tears flowing as Ching passed away smiling.

Soon an SUV arrived very fast, and it came to a halt just a few feet away from the group, and out stepped three masked Hunters. Marco and Matt removed their towels as the Hunters too removed their masks. One was a blond-haired, well-built man; the other, a beautiful lady with long blackish-brown pigtailed hair; and the third, a black-haired black man. They were in latex suits with the Hunter insignia on their chests. Their eyes were covered by pointed black domino masks. They looked at Marco and Matt and nodded. None spoke.

The blond one said, "We were in Washington, so we were late. Ching's men, and we're sorry we couldn't be here on time."

Marco just nodded with sadness.

The blond, with his comrades, picked up Ching's body and got into the SUV and, afterexchanging sad looks with Matt and Marco, said, "Shall meet later. Now's not the time for introduction and greetings. Never thought we'll be meeting in such a sad situation," then drove off.

Marco looked at the book and saw it had a sketch of a monstrous firefly now. He then got up and placed his stuff in his bag, and he left with Matt. Sadly they cycled back to their homes through the city and its rubbles.

But unknown to them, one of their classmates, a girl with long brownish-black hair and black eyes who was absent in class as she was out of town, had gotten separated from her relatives during the fuss created by the monster and had watched the climax of the monster attack unfolding. She was in tears upon witnessing the passing away of a good professor, Prof. Ching, and she looked at the SUV going away with Ching's body and at her classmates Matt and Marco looking at the book and then putting it—along with the sheathed sword and the flask with the liquid—into Marco's big navy-green bag and riding away from the shadows of a half-destroyed and toppled skyscraper, which had crashed slanting into a sideways skyscraper.

On the next day, Ching was known as dead to many. His identity of being a Hunter remained a secret. The blond, well-built man, Alex, and his two friends, Sasha and Martin, appeared as Ching's martial arts students, and they fabricated the story that it was on the day of their meeting that the firefly attacked. These three were trapped in a building with many others after they all ran for safety, but Ching had run into an ill-fated way, thus he breathed his last unfortunately.

Three days after the firefly attack, the school reopened, and it held the mourning for Ching. Later in class, a paper was found in Marco's drawer, written with "*I know the secret.*" Marco looked at it and just wondered who it was. Later during break, Matt also told him about a note he got in his drawer. Both became sure there was a third person in their class who knew about Ching's secret with them. But they thought that except for them, everyone believed Alex's fabricated story of Ching's death. They wondered who this person was.

Later that day after class, as Marco and Matt were sitting in Marco's room, Marco said, "One thing is for sure, whoever knows this isn't gonna be a trouble as they would have troubled us by now."

Matt also agreed.

On the next day, the same thing happened. And again, the same thing happened on the third day. Marco got irritated, and to counter-irritate the person, he wrote a note saying, "*So what? There is no prize offered if you know our secrets.*" The girl with long brownish-black hair saw Marco writing a note as a reply and placing it in his table's drawer, and as the class emptied, she quickly and cunningly went and took the note and read it and was mad at the reply and became irritated as Marco had assumed.

On the fourth day, nothing new happened, and it was like that for the rest of the week that followed. The girl meantime thought of going to Marco's house and getting an entry into this team of special supernatural hunters she had witnessed a few days before.

One fine day in the Yellowstone region, a fair reddish-haired girl of twenty years was strolling to kill her boredom. She went into a cave and was about to come out of it when she saw a strange gold chain shining, which was lying on a stone. She took it. It had a snake pendant on it. She took it happily and, without any second thought, stuffed it into her pocket and left happily.

Her mom and aunt saw the necklace after she wore it, and they asked how she got it. She told them she found it in a cave. After some time, they left that topic alone.

Later that night, her aunt said to her mother, "By living here, nothing's gonna happen. We have to venture out and live in the cities."

Her mom just listened, saying, "Hmmm . . ." She was nodding her head sadly in agreement when the girl replied rudely, "What's there to venture? Both of you and the others have no say in anything since one day we will be ruling the world"

Both women were shocked upon hearing such drastic words coming from her once-sweet mouth.

13

The girl went to sleep, and at midnight, the pendant glowed. The girl woke up with red eyes. Then she hissed, and three snakes came through the gaps in the walls. The mother and aunt, on hearing the sounds, came and were shocked to find the girl chatting—hissing—with three deadly cobras. They tried shouting for help, but their voices didn't come out in fear. The girl saw them, and they were trying to shout when she said in a strict, cold voice, "Can't you both shut up? What does it take to shut your mouths?"

She looked at the snakes, and the snakes looked at the women, hissing. They crawled at great speed and bit them and returned to their old positions; in less than two minutes, the girl's aunt and mom fell dead.

"*Silence* at last," whispered the girl, laughing and raising her hands into the air. Sitting on the bed, she said, "My dear ones, in the morning, come to the house and kill whoever comes in your way. Coz it's time we take over."

Every snake in the Yellowstone area hissed as they all heard the command in their heads.

On Sunday, the girl went to Marco's house, and even Matt was there.

On seeing the girl Rachel, who was the most gorgeous and hottest girl in their school coming to them, both were thrilled.

"Hi," said the boys.

"Hi," replied Rachel.

"What is it that we can do for you?" asked Matt.

Seeing Matt's sudden generosity, Marco looked at him, open-mouthed and in a bit of surprise.

"Actually . . ." said Rachel, "I saw your moments at Ching's death place. I came to ask you to include me as well in this team of yours, Hunters."

"So it was you," said Marco.

Rachel nodded.

"Look, dear," said Marco, "this is not some kind of dance team-up in our school, and we're just new to all this business and not sure how long we can hold on now that Ching too is not here."

"Yeah," said Matt a bit strictly and shyly, "even if he was here, you won't be taken in."

"But—" said Rachel.

"No buts and puts, dear," said Matt, and Marco nodded in agreement.

After lots of requests and pleadings to join the team, the boys were ready to give in.

"But—" said Marco.

Matt interrupted, looking at Rachel, "Okay, you are in."

"Hmm . . ." said Marco. "You'll have to keep up on your own."

"Oh yes, she will, and don't be a class prefect here too. Here, Marco's the prefect," said Matt.

"Yeah, yeah. Thanks," said Rachel, smiling.

Marco and Matt looked at each other.

"And as we three are in the same neighborhood," said Rachel, "we can hang out together too, and none would interfere or doubt us. And also I can help you with your class works."

"We can handle it by ourselves . . ." Matt dragged his sentence, then said quickly, "it'll still be better if you too can help us with it."

"But why are you so determined to join the team when it can cost you your life?" asked Marco, and Matt nodded as he too had the same question in mind.

"I once witnessed a terrible massacre. An innocent family living a few streets away were brutally killed by a goblin gang in front of the town. Even their small three-year-old boy was not spared," said Rachel with teary eyes.

"Hey, sorry, we had heard about it, and the Hunters caught the killers and had captured them and punished them," said both the boys in unison.

"Yeah, that too happened in this town itself, and from that time onward, I too wanted to be a Hunter to punish the wrongdoers. Well, I shall catch up with you both later. Gotta go. Otherwise, my mom would be worried if I get more late," said Rachel, "Never thought I'll have to come for an interview in front of two stupids like you both," She puffed up with pride.

"And the two stupids got the medal, you nerd loser," said Matt.

"Yeah, yeah," said Rachel, speeding off. "See you losers tomorrow in class."

Marco shrugged his shoulders and said, "Let her come, and she herself will run back scared to her mommy when she realizes a job of a Hunter is not easy for people like her."

Matt smiled and said, "Yeah."

That evening, there was news on various channels on the strange behavior of snakes. When they heard the news, the trio knew something supernatural was in play, but where and what it was, none of them even had a clue.

"I read it in some book that there might be a girl or a man behind this madness somewhere," said Rachel.

"And mostly they do."

"Great guess, dear," said Matt.

"There are about 7 to 8 million people in this city, and among them, who's the one we want?" said Marco.

"Sheesh . . ." said Rachel, biting her tongue on having realized the stupidity in her assumption and lowering her head ashamedly.

Matt said lowly, teasingly, "Maybe the brightest girl is not so bright after all."

Rachel heard that and said, "Oh, shut up."

Marco laughed.

The next day, as the three of them were passing a garden on their way back from school, they spotted a young gal of their age with reddish-black hair, sitting, wearing tribal clothing on the soft, trimmed, grassy ground. And around her were snakes.

"I think we have found the cause, but where are the guards to stop the snakes in the park?" said Marco, looking for a guard.

"Um . . ." said Matt, pointing to the bushes on his left. "No use in looking as they have already interfered and are now gone."

Marco and Rachel looked in the direction Matt was pointing ahead of him, and they saw three dead guards lying on the ground, half hidden by the rose bushes. Marco, Matt and Rachel stood behind a tall trees adjoining the bush.

Marco and Matt were about to shout to the woman when Rachel put her hands over their mouths and pulled them back.

Matt and Marco said, "What are you doing?"

Rachel dug her hands into her side pockets and took out small thumb-sized disks, gave the disks to them, and said, "Press that green dot on it."

They did, and suddenly, some kind of matter covered them entirely and quickly, and soon they were wearing red latex suits covering even their faces and hair. On their chests, they had an orange Hs insignia in a circle with a lightning bolt behind it.

"Cool . . ." said Matt, "But the font's different in the original and red in color. Now we stand out like a damaged traffic signal with green and red lights missing."

"Thanks, Rachel, and so much for your fashion tips, dear Matt. Let's discuss that later. Now let's get back to work," said Marco, and both the boys came out through the opening, with Marco holding a sword.

A park stroller saw them, and he ran back to the gate, scared.

Marco took out the items while Rachel decided to create a distraction if the girl attacks and Matt took his pen and threw it at the girl, disturbing her.

"You are just some psycho with a strange power who had come here to irritate the world," shouted Matt, annoying her.

The girl commanded the snakes to attack them. Rachel used a sharp rod and threw it at the electric lines. The lines got cut and fell down. It electrified the water already splashed on the grass, and the snakes attacking Marco and Matt were electrified.

Rachel went toward the boys as she and the boys tied their hankies around their faces like thieves. Rachel shouted at the girl, "Whoever you are, you are nothing to us."

Marco told Rachel in a soft tone, "Keep quiet, and don't challenge her till we are sure what we're dealing with."

Just then, the girl got angry and lifted herself in the air a bit and then flew toward the trio.

"Hmm . . ." said Matt, looking at the other two, "Too late, mates."

The girl neared them and hit them hard with an invisible force shield, sending them crashing backward to the ground.

Marco threw a bit of the liquid, but it bounced off an invisible shield. He looked at her, surprised.

"I'm Carolina, and I am now this world's queen," said the lady.

"Ms. Carolina!" exclaimed Rachel. "Why didn't you try to slash her?" She looked at Marco, and Matt nodded, supporting her question.

"I can't attack a girl," said Marco. "Thought she might make it easy by transforming her looks into some hideous demon as we see in cartoons."

"Oh how very sweet of you," said Rachel and seized the sword from Marco's hand. "This is the wrong time for your morals, Mr. Righteous, Better I take the sword now, or we'll be dead soon. You do what needs to be done."

"Okay," said Marco, "but be careful. Just cut her once, and I'll do the rest with the book."

"I know, I had seen the Hunters at work," said Rachel and got up with a threatening look at the girl.

"Hmm," said Matt as she went running, then stood her ground, brandishing the sword as she faced Carolina, challenging her, "she's quite proud."

Marco smirked.

Carolina came at her, running, as Rachel readied herself. Rachel blocked Carolina's attack with her invisible force shield.

"She's good," admitted Matt, watching her blocking well.

Rachel defended herself well against Carolina's attacks.

"Now my turn to attack," said Rachel mockingly, and she attacked the girl. The girl defended herself well, but then while backing off, she tripped on her leg and fell, and as she fell, Rachel's attack found a mark.

The boys saw it, and Marco came forward and opened the book. As wind and lightning occurred, the girl was dragged into the pages, and a sketch of the girl with a green snake curled around her neck and wearing a snake pendant was formed.

Rachel looked at the sketch. Walking up to them, Matt said, "That cut was a lucky one."

Rachel stuck out her tongue and said, "At least I was able to help capture her."

"Well, all's well again," said Marco. There was the sound of sirens approaching. They went behind a bush and pressed the red dot on the disks as Rachel said, and they were switched back to their normal looks. They then raced out via the other gate.

"Okay, we gotta run," said Marco. "We're already late."

The trio rode into the street with their cycles and went off to their homes.

"Well, you know sword fights," said Marco to Rachel on the way.

"Oh . . ." said Rachel, smiling, "it was nothing. I don't really know it, just a bit to help in a fight that's all. But I was worried you would have your no-attacking-girls opinion again before getting the book to trap her."

The trio laughed and sped up. Marco said, "Maybe I should reconsider my earlier opinion on having you join us, it looks like we could really use some help from you . . . before it's too late."

They all laughed again.

At Marco's house after two normal months, the trio arranged a meeting and were staring at their study books when Matt said, "Man, it's been two months now, but no adventure. I wish we'll have an adventure soon."

Rachel said, "Idiot, don't wish for anything."

Matt said, "It's just a wish."

"Some come true when you least expect it," said Rachel.

"Yeah," said Marco, "I too have heard that saying."

"Hey, come on, you guys," said Marco. "What can happen? Those are just stories, and moreover, we're the Hunters, and we can deal with anything thrown at us."

Very early the next day at 3 a.m., a lady with bits of witchcraft knowledge released three ghosts by mistake while using a spell to talk with her dead husband. They turned her household upside down and went out and inhabited the first building that came in their way. It was the MU, and they started wreaking havoc all over the place. After two hours, everyone came and was shocked to find the mess in the school.

Just then, one of them spotted a ghost moving through walls and doors, not noticing the students. She screamed in fright, and everyone looked at her. Others saw the ghost too, and it too saw them. Hearing the commotions, the other two ghosts arrived from outside, and all the kids and staff were scared to be cornered by the three ghosts. They ran, scared. The ghostly trio scared them into the library room.

One of the ghosts, a young man with pony tailed, curtained hairs randomly caught a fat kid, who happened to be a bully to other kids, and threw him out of the window, but he held on to a pole, wetting his pants in fright.

Marco had had enough.

"But how will we stop them when they are spirits?" said Rachel.

"Good question," said Marco, "but sitting here is useless. We gotta try."

He opened his bag and took out the flask and applied the liquid on the sword.

"You don't need it, do you?" asked Matt.

"Who knows? We are facing ghosts for the first time," said Marco. And he got up and shouted, "Hey!"

Everyone looked at him. Marco brandished the sword at the ghosts. The fat one of the ghostly trio, who had curly brown hair, came forward, laughing mockingly.

"You think you can scare us?" He laughed and touched the sword with force, but instead of passing through the sword, his hand hit the sword. Some of the liquid on the sword got applied to his hand and it developed a small cut.

"Wow, this sword even cuts a ghost!" said Marco, surprised and beaming with I-got-payback-in-store-for-you eyes.

Marco saw that somehow the liquid had stuck to the ghost's fist. He opened the book, and everyone saw the fat ghost being pulled into the book. Everyone was surprised. In fear, the other two ghosts passed through the floor to the basement below as Rachel and Matt got up too, ready to fight beside Marco, and accompanied him in chasing them.

All others sat with fear in the library itself. None attempted to run out as all their legs couldn't move with fright. But they all knew now that the three were indeed Hunters.

At the basement, Marco wondered a bit loudly with the other two how they were gonna face the rest of the school.

"Now how do we explain our secrets of being new Hunters?"

Rachel said, "Leave that to me."

"What do you mean?" asked the boys together.

"Maybe I can as I got a spray my scientist parents made. With this spray, one will forget the last one hour in one's life," said Rachel.

"Wow," said the boys.

"Mom and Dad said," Rachel said, "this spray somehow affects the brain and destroys the cells that collect the data. I keep one as I am a girl and to save myself from the kidnappers by erasing the memories of the last one hour in their lives and making them unable to focus and sleepy for ten minutes, in which I can make my escape. And moreover, after two minutes, the liquid outside the can evaporates."

"Kidnappers?" Matt said.

"My dad now has many enemies after he took over as the leader of the recent solar project," said Rachel.

"Wow," said both the boys.

"Okay," said Marco.

"Now let's end this, and moreover, we just have to splash the liquid at them, and I just gotta slash the sword once as it can even hurt ghosts too," said Marco, and the trio went to the basement to catch the ghostly duo.

"Let's go," said Matt. "It's time the ghosts ran from humans, ha ha ha."

"That's true," said Marco.

"Hmm . . ." said Rachel, "a new theory to try and maybe the last if it fails."

The basement was too dark, and all of a sudden, a builder-like ghost with curly brown hair caught Matt by the foot, holding him upside down. Marco and Rachel tried throwing the liquid at the ghost in small quantities but failed as the ghost moved here and there, and the ghost laughed mockingly, avoiding the liquid preventing it from touching him.

Just then, Matt smiled and, taking a small test tube holding the potion from his pocket, splashed the liquid on the ghost. He looked at Marco and yelled, "Now."

In anger, the ghost picked up Marco.

Marco took the book and opened it, and the ghost dropped Matt for throwing the liquid at him and got sucked into the book opened by Marco just in time.

Matt looked at the figure on the book and said, "We all are equipped, thankfully."

Marco and Rachel smiled.

With two gone, they searched for the third. Just then, a shelf with many tools and boxes fell on them, and the test tube of the liquid rolled off a bit far after Marco lost his hold on it. Even the sword went and fell near Rachel. They saw the third ghost, which was that of a young man with a ponytailed, curtained hair, coming at them, brandishing a sword. But this sword seemed near to a real one, and they ducked in time as the sword went slashing the shelf and the few books in it.

Rachel took Marco's sword and blocked the attack when it came again at them, and then both started fighting aggressively as Marco quickly got himself free from the fallen shelf.

Rachel suffered a cut on her arm, but she continued counterattacking and defending.

In the meantime, Matt freed himself from the shelf that had fallen on them, and they came up from behind and surprised the ghost by splashing the liquid on his face. The ghost had not noticed the other two getting free. The ghost looked at Matt, who was facing him. Matt opened the book, and the ghost was sucked in just like his partners.

They all looked at the pages, and in them, the sketches were formed, each ghost's sketch covering two continuous pages. After looking at it, they decided to go upstairs and meet the others in the library.

Meanwhile, in the library, all people were talking of Matt, Rachel, and Marco being associated with the mysterious Hunters. On the way, Rachel took out the spray and sprayed it in the air, and to help the spray spread out Marco used the sword and created a wind he self-learned after watching Ching's moves at the firefly a few months before. All people in the library were sprayed with the wind's help.

After ten minutes, everyone looked normal but wondered what they all were doing in the library, and none remembered anything else. Marco, Matt, and Rachel acted as if they too were there just like the others.

The trio looked at each other and smiled.

Just then, everyone heard a shout saying, "How did I get here? Someone get me down."

They all went to the left side of the building and saw Fat Jack holding on to a strong pole.

"How did you get there?" asked a student.

"That we can talk later, anyone get me out of here," cried out Jack.

After a few minutes, everything was back to normal.

"Wow," said Rachel, "good thing he held on. Otherwise, he would have been history."

"Yeah," said Marco, "good thing he held on. Strange thing no one thought about him when we were in the basement."

"Nah," said Rachel, "in fear of those ghosts, even he might have not bothered to shout for help, and the others, thinking he's dead, might have been scared to even look for him with the ghosts still down."

"Hmm . . ." said Marco, "they had even closed the doors and windows so none could go out, I guess."

"Anyway, leave it," said Matt. "Now I'm never gonna wish anything out of normal. I had enough."

Rachel and Marco laughed.

Later, at Marco's tree house, they looked at the ghostly trio's pics.

Matt said, "How come the sketches are spread through two pages?"

Marco and Rachel said in unison, "Why?"

Matt said, "I was wondering if they too are folded inside this book. Wish we could see how it is inside.

"You stupid, not again," shouted Marco and Rachel.

Matt smiled, showing his teeth, and said, "He he . . . Hey, that's never gonna work. We're never going in that book coz that's a prison for the supernatural freaks we capture. And how are we gonna go in that? After all, we can't just open the book and jump in it."

HUNTERS

That night, a beast was released by an evil sorcerer to attack the city. The beast had three fanged heads with fiery red eyes and looked like a giant mutated wolf. It was known as the hellhound.

Two

The hellhound ransacked the house it was summoned in. It pounced and tore its evil master to pieces and ate him—the one who had summoned it—and then leaped out of the window, breaking the wall, and headed toward the city, ransacking everything in its path. It created a path of destruction in its wake. This beast was one of the dangerous and hard-to-tame beasts in the occult world. Its evil master foolishly thought he could tame it, and he paid the price for his try; now the beast is out in the world to wreak havoc.

The next day, on the news, the monster's rampage was the topic. The trio decided to face it at Central Park, which was in its path. They cycled toward the park very fast and waited after activating the Hunter suit created by Rachel, and just there was a black-haired black man, whom Marco remembered seeing standing next to Alex when he gave out the news of Ching's demise. He saw them and approached them. Marco introduced himself, saying as he took off his mask, "Hi . . . I'm Mr. Ching's student, Marco, and these too are his students and my best buddies, Matt and Rachel." Matt and Rachel removed their masks too.

He smiled and shook hands with them and said, "I'm Martin, and as I am in town for a few days, for a start, I thought of helping you in handling this. I knew you and the monster will ultimately come here."

"Hmm . . . Why's that?" said Marco. "And where are your pals?"

"They're in Belgium, visiting Mr. Ching's daughter, Jane, and I came here coz this park is just on its path," Martin said.

"Oh . . ." said Rachel, "Ching's daughter is in Belgium!"

"Hmm . . . I last saw her when she came for the funeral," said Matt.

"Yeah," said Marco.

Martin extended his hand to shake their hands again and said, "Glad to have met you three."

"Why is it so? You shook our hands earlier," asked Rachel.

"So you don't know about our clan much, do you?" asked Martin.

"What do you mean?" said Matt. "Why do you say so?"

Just then, a car went flying and crashed into a skyscraper. The monster had arrived in the city. It was a giant mutated beast.

"Well . . ." said Martin, drawing his sword ahead and putting on a black domino mask, "shall tell later." Ready to fight, he stood along with the trio, who too had donned their masks.

The Hunters had their stuff ready. The hellhound saw the four humans standing to face it. It ran toward them to attack. Marco jumped forward with his sword, along with Martin. Matt ignored the rules to save the potion and sprayed the liquid in its path so that they could capture it easily.

Marco saw this and shouted out, "What are you doing?"

"Don't waste it thus," said Marco.

"Mannn," said Rachel, "the look of that thing gives me the creeps, and better we don't follow the rules."

Marco struck its paw with his sword when it pounced, and then Rachel opened the book. But as the beast was sucked into the book, it stuck out its five snake-like lengthy tongues at them. Four tongues found each Hunter's leg and wrapped around them and pulled them toward its mouth while the fifth tongue wrapped around a mini car and pulled it toward its mouth as a slender young woman and a man leaped out of it. The Hunters tried hard to free themselves from the grip, but they too were pulled along with the beast into the book. The book fell on to the street.

The lady and the man saw the beast as it dragged the four Hunters into the book. They ran and took the book and ran among the halted vehicles into an alley. The traffic had been disturbed due to the monster. They stopped in the alley and opened it, and inside they saw ten pages with the beast's and the Hunters' sketches. Their faces were covered with masks. The beast's tongues were wrapped around the four Hunters' legs.

Meanwhile, in the book, the four spun and crashed to the ground and found themselves in a new environment.

"What happened?" asked Matt and Rachel as they removed their masks.

"Good news, we're alive . . . and bad news, we're in the prison realm," said Martin.

"What's that?" asked the trio in unison.

"That's the realm inside the book," said Martin, "the one where we trap these evil ones." There were many huge rocks, some with water bodies floating on air. The Hunters and the hellhound were on one such rock.

The sky had strange lines across it.

Matt said, "So if we're in the book and this is the world in the book, so those lines are the end of the pages, I guess?"

"Maybe . . . yeah, dude. You wanted to know how it is inside, well now you just found out," said Marco.

Rachel too looked at Matt and said, "Now never ever."

Matt showed his teeth and said, "He he . . . This is also just a coincidence."

And before they spoke anything else, Martin, pointing to the monster stirring up to stand on its legs, answered, "Before you ask anything more . . . I hate to say it, but none has been here before, so I don't know how to get back to New York."

Matt pointed to the lines and was about to speak when Martin interrupted, "Going up there is impossible coz we have enslaved flying monsters, and won't they have tried to reach it?"

The trio's hopes got shattered.

Just then the beast slowly stood up on its legs and bared its sharp teeth at the four humans. It was a new world in all, and they were on a far cliff on a land that floated in air. They saw the evils they had captured before on different rocks, heading to the rock they were on.

Carolina flew to a rock near them and said, "Well, well, well . . . what have we got here? The brats who spoiled our fun and imprisoned us. Ha ha ha ha ha ha ha."

The four stood ready to fight, but then suddenly, the beast pounced on the rock Carolina was standing on. Carolina, the snake lady, fell down and rose with anger and hissed at the beast. The beast stopped, showing its teeth at her.

Just then, out of the ground came a beast that looked like a snake like reddish-yellow dragon. It had a pair of scaly bat-like wings, and its body was covered with tiny scales like that of a fish. It had a pair of blood-red eyes and breathed green flame. It looked at the trio and said, "It's been a long time since we four had met."

The trio was shaking with fear, and deep within, they were already dead.

Shaking but without showing his fear, Matt said, "A dragon, great. When did we capture this one?"

Marco said bravely, "I don't think we were the ones who did."

The hellhound looked at the dragon fiercely. It was surprised to see a dragon after having been summoned.

The dragon, with its flame, destroyed the hellhound to pieces when it pounced at the beast.

"No one interrupts Dragoon," said the beast, roaring.

Meanwhile outside the book, the book glowed blue and orange. The man and woman opened the book to see that the beast that had dragged the humans had its sketch disappearing. The tongues around the Hunters' feet too disappeared.

"What just happened?" said the young woman.

The man looked at her with a puzzled look on his face.

Meanwhile, in the prison realm, the four hunters faced Dragoon.

"Okay," said Martin, "so you're Dragoon?"

"Do you know this Dragoon?" asked the trio in unison.

Dragoon, on hearing the trio's puzzled question, laughed wildly.

"Actually," said Martin, "you three should be knowing him too." And then seeing more puzzled looks on their faces, he completed it by saying, "In one way or another, I guess."

"We have met almost 2,100 years before . . . if I'm right. It was you three who imprisoned me," said Dragoon, and he fired a deadly fire beam.

The Hunters ran. Matt spotted a small passage between the two giant rocks, and he ran toward it. Others followed him.

They found an opening toward an underground lake. They went into the passage.

Meantime, the ghosts and the snake lady volunteered to go into the passage, and Dragoon waited outside as the others went after them, just in case the Hunters came out outwitting them.

Meantime, a bit far away on another drifting mass of land, the mutated firefly flew.

After ten minutes in the passage, the Hunters found a large portal. It was a large open portal. The hunting party saw the Hunters. They flew toward them at a good speed to catch them, but their speed was more than they expected; they crashed onto the four Hunters, and unexpectedly, all eight went into the portal.

They all came crashing into a slope near a fiery pit. Dragoon saw all eight crashing in a nearby drifting mass. So did the firefly. Both flew toward them from their respective drifting landmasses.

They all went rolling down the slope and into the waters of another landmass below it.

All eight surfaced here and there on the shores of the lake. But luckily, the Hunters were together, and their rivals were on the other end. The rivals began to fly toward the Hunters. The Hunters ran into the woods.

"Wow," said Matt, "those portals are doors for traveling between these landmasses."

A few feet before them, there were blue lights coming from a cave. The four Hunters saw it and ran toward it. It was another portal. They ran in and came out to a forest on another floating landmass. Soon they began searching for portals and jumping from one landmass to another. Then Marco said, "We gotta quit following the map if we have to outwit them."

"You mean . . . ?" said Martin.

"Portals open in one direction, and we go jumping from one to another, and they keep chasing us. Instead of going onto any different landmass, we eight end up in the same one," said Marco. "So why don't we jump across to the next one while they go through portals into some other landmass?"

"Cool," said Matt.

"But we need water below if we are to jump to a landmass below ours and a short distance between the landmasses if we're jumping across," said Rachel.

"Or," said Martin, pointing to the waterfall to the side, "let's hide there and hope they won't find us."

Dragoon and the firefly were flying toward the landmass where they got a glimpse of the chasers. Luckily, the chasers didn't bother to look the entire landmass and went into a portal to another landmass.

"Well," said Rachel, looking at Martin, "now tell us everything."

Martin looked at Marco and Matt and the looks on their faces, which said that they too had the same thing to say.

"Well," said Martin, "it began almost 2,100 years ago when the Hunter clan was formed. Believe it or not, but you three started it."

"What?" said the trio in unison and with amazement and wonder on their faces.

Martin said, "Many years before, in a war between Queen Akilo of another universe and Dragoon, it all thus began. Queen Akilo's three trusted soldiers fought Dragoon and almost defeated him. So in order to win, he opened up a portal to another universe, or realm, as we say. Three of his evil wizard allies helped him in recreating the portal necessary for the universal leap into a realm which he could terrorize and where he could create an army and come back to terrorize Queen Akilo's realm. Queen Akilo was also a spell-weaver in their realm. These three and Queen Akilo followed Dragoon one fine day."

"She was a sorceress?" said Matt.

"Nope, she wasn't one, but she knew how to create some spells. She was a minor version of a sorceress, which is a spell-weaver, in one way," Martin said.

All three listened without bothering about anything as the search for them went on.

The firefly was searching for the Hunters as it could kill and eat something lively and won't have to struggle.

Earlier, it had attacked Dragoon, but Dragoon had defeated it then. And so it feared Dragoon. And the others were always with Dragoon, so it didn't dare to attack them too.

"But Queen Akilo in the meantime fell in love with a warrior and, using some spell, gave him long life," continued Martin, "a very long life. She even gave birth to a beautiful girl. But one day, Queen Akilo, her three trusted soldiers and the warrior, all five chased Dragoon back. And after three days' war, Dragoon hurt Queen Akilo, who passed away on the fourth day. In anger, they tried to kill Dragoon, but here again; Dragoon had a sort of help as his three faithful wizards stood in between. Queen Akilo's soldiers managed to fight them as Queen Akilo's husband chased Dragoon. The trio, however, couldn't make it out alive as the wizards were too powerful, and they died in the portal to the newfound realm.

"Few nights after catching some spooks on his way back, Queen Akilo's husband saw the wizards and Dragoon. He hid behind a rock, and he heard of the fate of the three warriors. One of the wizards told Dragoon that since they were killed in the path to the new realm, they could be born again in the new realm. That man heaved a sigh of relief for the first time after losing his wife and three pals as that new realm was the one in which he too lived. He wanted Dragoon to die in the hands of those three, and so he sprang up a sudden attack. The wizards were taken by surprise, and they bled under his sharp samurai sword. Dragoon too got a cut. He captured Dragoon and that's where we are now."

"But what does it have to do with us?" said Rachel and Marco.

"Unless this is the new universe, or realm," said Matt, putting the pieces together.

"What!" said Marco and Rachel in unison.

"Exactly," said Martin. "That man didn't know how to go to their realm, and for him, this is his realm. And moreover, those three warrior pals will be reborn because they were killed in the path to this realm, as he had heard one of the dark wizards tell Dragoon."

"And where are they and that man?" asked Marco.

"That man is dead, and the other three are . . ." said Martin pointing to the trio's reflection on the water of the underground lake beside them.

The trio looked at him pointing. But they saw nothing but their reflections. After a few seconds, all three shouted in wonder at the same time, "No way!"

Martin nodded and said, "You three are that Hunters, and the realm from which we came to this prison realm is not your actual realm."

The trio didn't say anything when Martin said, "Mr. Ching was that warrior who had been gifted the long life by Queen Akilo."

"But . . ." said Matt.

Meanwhile, at the alley, the man was flipping through the pages and looking at the sketches. The gal peeped by leaning across his shoulder and said, "John, what's this book?"

"No idea, but this looks like something from the Hunters," said John.

"Those four and that beast just vanished into the book," said the gal. "Were they the Hunters?"

Just then, a fat man and two medium-built men showed up. They had a rough biker gang's look. The fat man snatched the book from John's hands, flipped the pages, and tossed it backward, saying, "Sweethearts, give us all your damn valuables, and then you can continue to see your stupid book."

The pages with the Hunter's sketch were torn off the book, and some kind of electricity ran across the pages and into the air.

All of them looked. The bullies turned around on hearing the crackling electricity sounds.

Before the pages touched the ground, some kind of blue plasma energy flew out of it and formed into three men and a woman. And then with a final crack of electricity, the forms materialized. Marco, Matt, Martin, and Rachel were back in their realm.

The four looked at the bullies and the couple. On seeing Marco and Martin wielding swords, the bullies ran off in fear, shouting, "Aaaaaaah . . ."

"Don't worry, and thanks," said Martin to the couple, and along with the trio, they ran out of the big dim alley as the couple looked puzzled.

Marco, Rachel, and Matt were done for the day. Just then, Martin, who was checking his cell, said, "Well, my cell's network came on, and I just received a message from the other Hunter, Alex, and seventy-five missed calls. Wow!"

"And . . . ?" said Rachel.

"Alex and the other Hunter, Sasha, and Ching's daughter, Jane, are coming in tonight's flight."

"Okay," said Matt.

"Tomorrow," said Martin, "you three come to Jane's place. We should talk."

"Yeah," said Marco, "let us all rest after that visit to that absurd territory."

Martin showed a thumbs up and winked, and the trio sped their bikes to their homes to rest after a tiring visit to the prison realm as Martin had said.

The next day, all three met at Rachel's place after breakfast at their homes, and all three sped their bikes to Ching's place. In the meantime, Martin and the others just had their breakfast and were sitting on the lawn under a giant oak, awaiting the arrival of the trio. Martin told everything to his comrades—a blond stud named Alex, a ponytailed blond, Sasha, and Jane, who has long black hair. They were excited to meet the trio.

They entered, one after another—first Marco, followed by Rachel, and then Matt.

Jane looked a bit amazed and said, "Never thought I'll see the Hunter clan's founders. So welcome, founders." The trio looked a bit shocked to know Jane knew about them.

Martin smiled and said, "I told them everything."

"You guys don't worry," said Jane. "Have something to eat first, and you are our guests."

"Thanks, but no thanks," said Rachel. "We just had our breakfast."

"Okay, let us sit down and talk," said Alex. "By the way, I'm Alex, and"—he indicated the other girl—"this is Michelle. You can call her Sasha too."

Meantime, Jane offered each of them some cool lemonade, which the trio took after saying thanks.

Jane said, "I'm the daughter of Ching and Queen Akilo of Realm 001, as we few say, a realm once terrorized by an evil beast Dragoon as far as I know," said Jane.

"Yeah," said Martin teasingly, "Princess Jane!"

"Shut up, Marty," Jane said.

"Yes, Your Highness," said Martin as he and Alex cracked a laugh.

Yeah, I know that what I'm gonna say now is hard for you to digest . . ." Jane said, without paying attention to them. "Yes, you three and Dragoon are not of this realm. Dragoon had somehow opened a way to a new realm to rule, and you, all along with my mom, chased him. As for you four, if he had a realm of his own, you lot wouldn't allow him to terrorize the freedom of the innocents no matter what it took. And in one such chase, my mom died, and in the tunnel bridging both the realms, you three too died. Now as your lives were destroyed in the tunnel, your soul energies were cast out into this realm, and so you were reborn here. As my dad assumed, the soul energies might have taken some time to collect together.

And looking at Rachel she said "You are Marissa" then looking at the boys she continued "and one of you is Kyle and other is Jordan, but who is who only my dad knew. "You lots were here for the first time some 2,130 years before, and I was born 2,129 years ago. Now dad's not an expert about that tunnel or soul energies, so he doesn't know. Dad, after defeating Dragoon, held up the Hunter legacy. The Hunter legacy at that time was just a group of three people that you three named to hunt down Dragoon. Like we have FBI and CIA, you three created Hunters—or what some of us call Hs, as you three first called it—which you gave to Ching. But later after your demise, my dad expanded it to fight evil, supernatural forces here, like the group at your home realm. He kept the name to honor you three. And you had hunted Dragoon, who too was evil, so he used that very name to fight the evil and even had me trained well. I myself was a Hunter but only for a very short period, unfortunately."

"What happened!" asked Rachel.

"I—" said Jane, looking at Martin and the others, "We four and my dad once fought a gargoyle who cursed me into a statue for more than two millenniums."

"What?" said Rachel. "Whoa . . . whoa . . . whoa . . . wait a minute. You are telling us that you all and your dad fought this gargoyle about two millenniums ago, then how come they are still young when only your time was stopped?"

Even Matt and Marco backed it by nodding.

"I never said that only I was turned to statue," said Jane.

"You mean . . . ?" said the trio in unison.

"Yeah," said Michelle, "we all were novices and were distracted, and so we were also turned into statues. That was a dark time for Hunters. Ching tried to get us back, but there was no other way but to wait, and during this wait, he recruited new members and expanded the group to fight evil."

"Why didn't your dad make the gargoyle free you?" said Rachel.

"He tried, and so he didn't give it a quick death, but that gargoyle was an adamant one too," said Jane.

"Like her dad," said Alex.

Jane continued, "He killed it one day after gaining its whereabouts, but before killing it, he even stripped its wings off and had it badly injured. He also used the suicide—breaker spell, which he had learned from my mom."

Alex said, "And many came, and many fell, except Ching, before we were freed. Also, he knew that you will be back, and so he trapped Dragoon in a blank book, like he had kept that gargoyle as a prisoner for some time. He saved him for you as he remembered the talk he had overheard between the wizards and Dragoon about your possible rebirth. You three were saying that one day you three will kill Dragoon as you were his friends long back. And he too hoped that since Dragoon was a good friend before, if he dies in his one-time friends' hands, he may live again in some realm as a good one."

"What! Our pal?" said Marco and Rachel, horrified.

"Yes! But that story even my dad didn't know as you lots never told him, nor had my mom ever hinted at anything about this," said Jane.

"Couldn't he free you by killing the gargoyle?" asked Marco.

"Hmm . . . nope, as this was no ordinary spell. As for this spell, we could only be freed if all 21 gargoyles that created this spell were killed as each has contributed a century in the lasting duration of the spell," said Sasha. "And so her dad hunted them down as fast as he can."

Jane said, "He couldn't find them as they were good in hiding, and for those that he could find, he couldn't defeat them as they were mostly too powerful. But after almost a millennium had passed, he freed us. And in our old culture, it's said that when an evil one dies in the hand of his pal or a close one who's a good one, he may have peace in his afterlife. It's the same in many cultures. So Dad had Dragoon captured in the book he gave to you, Marco, and he glued those three pages with Dragoon's sketch so that he can tell you later, but unfortunately, my dad didn't live to say all this himself."

"Yeah," said Martin, looking at Marco, "so after he found out your time has come to become Hunters, he had already made us promise to tell this to you if he is not able to do so."

The trio listened carefully and looked at the faces of each of their new friends and then at each other in amazement.

"Okay," said Marco, "but what is this potion that weakens them?"

"That," said Jane, "is a substance made by mixing some spells you three taught Dad, who later taught us. It's like holy water of sorts. Your real realm had some inventions for keeping the evils at bay."

After a few hours, the trio left for their respective houses, taking their leave. Learning more about the original story was more tiring than a day of fighting any supernatural.

After a few days, Jane gifted Matt and Rachel two spare swords, which some deceased Hunters had used long ago. After a month, on one fine day, the skies darkened. A gigantic portal opened up, and out came a long dragon, just like Dragoon, but reddish green. It began searching for Dragoon, and on not seeing him, it began to wreak havoc. Few towers were destroyed. There was mayhem everywhere.

"If my brother is not here, then he might have lost, and now I'll rule here," roared the new dragon.

Rachel and the others were on a group conversation on the cell as they all were scattered. Marco was with his dad on a golf course; Rachel, shopping with her mom in a mall; Matt, with his engineer brother at a construction site; Jane, Alex, and Martin, on a seaside; and Sasha, buying some dresses.

"Now who the heck is this?" said Rachel.

"And why does he look just like Dragoon?" said Marco.

"I just heard him roaring. He's Dragoon's younger brother," said Matt.

"What?" said the rest in unison.

The new dragon flew and coiled on top of the Empire State Building from the outside and roared and breathed fire into the sky.

The US defense forces advanced toward the building in land as well as air.

Then, as if this wasn't enough, goblins entered. The goblins' leader advanced toward the new dragon by climbing to the top of the building, the dragon saw him and breathed fire. The goblin hid behind a wall in fear and shouted, "Your Highness, we are your humble servants."

"How can I trust you?" roared the dragon.

"Your brother, Lord Dragoon, was our ruler until the Hunters destroyed him and scattered us," said the goblin king, still hiding.

"Hunters . . . here too?" said Shenron.

The goblin king gathered his might and came from behind the wall and said, "Yes, Your Highness."

The goblin king told him how the original three Hunters died and how their new friend exacted revenge.

The dragon thought, *Maybe I can use these pests when the Hunters of this realm charge at me, so I should get them on my side.*

"Okay now, as my dear brother isn't here, I'm your new master. And get the Hunters one after the other in front of me, and I'll burn them. Now I, Shenron, am your master."

"Yes, my Lord Shenron," said the goblin king.

Meantime, Sasha was returning to Jane's place after they all agreed to meet there. She was driving the car swiftly when at a turn she spotted an alley shining with shimmering blue lights for a moment. She watched as she saw three blond men and two blond women come out into the streets. The men were wearing black T-shirts and navy-blue jeans while the women were wearing blue miniskirts and white tops. Each wore a broad steel-plated wristband on their right hands.

"Well, that's some kind of attraction," said Sasha to herself, and then she spotted the swords hanging in sheaths from each waist.

"I gotta say," said Sasha to herself as she turned her car toward them, "I think today is gonna be a great day!" and she whistled to herself.

Three

Shenron was proving to be invincible, and the goblins were now terrorizing on a large scale. Sasha arrived at Jane's house. Jane and the others were waiting for Sasha when her BMW SUV sped into the house. Out alighting from it were Sasha and five strangers.

"This is Mike," said Sasha, introducing a short blond-haired man, who was the fairest of the strangers, and she began introducing each one, "This here is Steve," introducing a long-haired blond, "this is Andrews," introducing a curly-haired blond, "this is Stella," introducing a short-haired blond, "and this is Maria," introducing a long-haired blond. "And they are Hunters-cum-portal-authorized-officers, or PAO, from another universe. This is Jane, Martin, Alex, Rachel, Matt, and Marco." Sasha also introduced them to her new friends.

"In short, this meeting is between the Hunters of two different dimensions as the dragon that's here is from their realm," said Sasha on seeing the blank faces of Martin, Jane, Alex, Matt, Marco, and Rachel.

They all greeted each other, and then, looking at Rachel, Steve began, "You three are legends in our dimension, those great Hunters whom none ever heard from again after they and Queen Akilo went after Dragoon. Nor did anyone hear about Dragoon. We all thought maybe both groups had succumbed—at least, till a few hours ago."

"What do you mean exactly?" asked Matt.

Steve said, "I mean, she's Marissa," pointing to Rachel, "you're Jordan," pointing to Matt, "and you're Kyle," pointing to Marco. Pointing to Jane, he said, "And you, Jane, you don't have any other name, but you have a very different title. As Michelle told us, you are Queen Akilo's daughter, and so you are a princess in our realm and is rightfully a queen. We have your threes statues in our headquarters to honor you."

They all looked at Jane.

"A real princess among us!" said Martin and Matt in unison, looking at each other, open-mouthed in surprise.

Looking at Michelle, Steve continued, "She told us only half of the story."

Looking at Rachel, Maria began, "Luckily, Dragoon is still a captive as Sasha told us, but unfortunately, now his brother, Shenron, is here."

"But Michelle told us something incorrect on our way," said Stella.

"And what would it be?" Matt said, looking at Michelle just like the others.

Michelle said, "I assumed Rachel, Marco, and Matt are from their universe. These three are neither from theirs nor ours as I thought. In fact, nor are Dragoon or Shenron. You five are from some totally different universe or realm."

"What!" said Jane, Alex, Martin, Rachel, Marco, and Matt.

Matt asked, "So where are we from if we're not from either of your universes?" He laughed faintly.

"In fact," said Maria, "we think you three are from what we call Realm 001."

Jane and the others opened their mouths.

"Yeah," said Mike, "Our realm is Realm 002, as we call our universe, and this is Realm 115 and not Realm 001, as you lot say. You three, Dragoon, and Shenron are from somewhere else out of the 126 universes or realms scattered, the one which we call Realm 001. Shenron once said that dreams and nightmares connect the realms together."

"There are 126 universes scattered across the space. It means," said Andrews, "we all have dreams or nightmares in which we're either running after someone—whether a stranger or someone we know—or swimming from a sinking ship in another or we have one in which our long-lost friends are meeting us or one in which they're fighting a revolution, and so on."

"It's just that," said Stella, "when we're asleep, our unconscious minds get scattered all over the realms, and we are just seeing what's happening or had happened or is gonna happen, and in some cases, it's really just our minds' tricks."

Steve said, "I dream I'm fighting with one of my friends or someone whom I don't know very well. That fight is something that will happen or is happening or has happened with my other self in some parallel realm. And we may be older or younger to our other selves."

"So," said Marco, looking at Mike as the others just pondered over the theories, "how can it be related, or does it have anything to do with our real realm if we're not from yours as well as theirs?" He looked at Martin.

Mike said, "You see, the relation of you three and this realm theory is that, as per the legend, you five—that is, you three, Shenron, and Dragoon—exploited such a possibility and thus you came to our realms."

"We exploited?" said Matt and Rachel in unison.

"Yeah, you," said Stella. "As per the story we know, you five were allies, but when you came to our world, Dragoon and Shenron were overpowered by the possibility of being rulers. Different thinking arose among you five, and your friendship broke. The Hunters—you three—killed Shenron in one duel. He later was reborn after a millennium or after a few years in the same realm he died. That is ours by coincidence. Maybe he was born somewhere else and might have died or not. We don't know."

Martin looked at Matt and said, "So that's the windup story or recap story about you three being their pals."

Sasha said, "Very true friends."

Matt said, "Well, that explains why two similar dragons exist in some of the dreams I have of us three hiking or adventuring. In some, we five are friends or enemies or strangers!"

Marco looked at Matt and Rachel and then at Sasha, Jane, and Maria.

"When one dreams in his or her sleep he or she is actually witnessing a past, present or a future they are gonna have in their next birth But the births or rebirths themselves can take place from one day to a million years," said Maria. "A new life unfolds."

"Yeah," said Andrews, "but sometimes you may meet a look-alike too or see a realm where you have lived once. But the fact is, unlike the reborn self, you don't have memories of any of the lives before, or after a particular one, no matter how fast or slow the rebirth is."

Jane and the others were fully spellbound to know this connecting theory of dreams, nightmares, birth, and rebirth.

"And here I was thinking that dreams are just not so real until now. They are fully complicated—in fact, more complicated than the lectures in school," said Matt, sighing.

"None have been able to travel between these realms until you five friends did it and that too by accident as you all then claimed, and we also later believed it as you all could have easily finished all the pending duties you lots used to speak of," said Mike.

"You mean . . . ?" asked Rachel.

"They have good memory. It took time, but they rewrote down all the procedures before their friendships cracked, and whereabouts you three were lost until now," said Stella.

Mike said, "One day a dragon called Grajulon stumbled upon one of these records, and he later learned the history which too had been recorded down in some manuscripts. After a lot of hard work and research, he recreated the travel, but then it was for his evil desire to rule. And he later took on his old life's name, Shenron."

Andrews said, "Shenron's fortress was attacked by us, but we were late by a few hours. Two of his five evil disciples opened it for us after having a small vengeful thought on their minds. Long before, Shenron was the reason they lost everyone they loved when he attacked one of our cities before he found the cave with procedures and techniques and history."

"Sweet," said Michelle. When others looked at her, she said with a wink and a wicked smile, "The disciples, I mean."

Others laughed.

"So how did Shenron make the travel between the realms possible?" asked Marco.

Stella said, "These five found out that there were more than three realms, and they genuinely prepared notes and stored them in their backpacks and later in a cave after visiting our realm. One of them, few centuries ago, gave our superiors every detail before the split started. And the real Shenron's magical friends can live on if no one kills them. The ability to live long until anyone kills them was

Shenron's gift to them for standing with him. They had a hand in reviving Shenron's past, some assume, and it was two of those friends who helped us. The portal-traveling details are now in safe hands—except for the one through which he came here, which he alone possessed.

"The traveling between these realms is supervised," said Andrews. "In fact, you can say it is banned."

Marco, Matt, and Rachel returned by 4 p.m. They felt they had been hit by a heavy cementing truck. They had too much info for a day that turned their universe, or at least the present universe, topsy-turvy. For a long time in their lives, they thought there was only one universe, and then after meeting Martin, they were told there is one more, and then just a few hours ago, they learned there is not just one or two but one twenty six in all.

Just then, four goblins attacked them all of a sudden. It was a random attack, and it was going on throughout the world. The goblins just snatched the bags and left. Luckily, the sword was in the sheath on Marco's hip, so the sword wasn't lost to them, but all other items were lost. The goblins didn't have any certain goal but were just snatching and running very fast. The Hunters didn't use their swords as they didn't want suspicion to arise regarding Hunters and them.

"Oh, no," said Marco, "damn it, we lost the items required to capture them except for the swords, which are attached to our belts and inner tees."

"Wonder why these freaks took our bag," said Rachel, checking the sword by running her hand on her jacket.

"Hope no more bad events happen," said Matt, sighing.

Rachel alone looked at him, open-mouthed.

The goblins each piled all the stolen objects together on a road below the Empire State Building.

Shenron, who had coiled up the top of the Empire State Building, glared furiously at the goblins piling up the objects below and flew toward them. When he passed by the pile, he fired a blazing flame at it. The pile began to burn. Shenron landed near it and roared, "You silly no-gooders are wasting time. Instead of finding this realm's pesky Hunters, you are stealing loots here."

Just then, there was a blue flash, and from the flash came out a gigantic monstrous firefly, a lady, three ghosts, and Dragoon.

"We're out," roared Dragoon.

"Brother!" roared Shenron in surprise. "You're alive."

"Master," said the goblins with joy and surprise on their faces.

"Of course I am," said Dragoon.

"I heard the Hunters are here too, and I thought you might have—" Shenron stopped with a murr.

"I'm glad you found your way back after your death, and now we'll rule this realm together as we had thought of earlier and kill those Hunters," said Dragoon.

Everyone stared at the dragon siblings. Both the dragons shrunk to their near-human forms. Dragoon wore a yellow cloth tied around his waist down to his knees and had a long spiky tail, and Shenron wore a green cloth tied around his waist down to his knees and had an identical long spiky tail. The brothers hugged each other.

Meanwhile, throughout the world, the news spread like a wildfire. Now all people feared what their fate would be. One brother was already wreaking havoc, and in the meantime, another brother arrived with a monstrous mutant firefly, three ghosts, and a snake lady with an ability to fly just a few feet above the ground and a disastrous power to command snakes.

"And now what?" They all wondered!

"Could this get any worse?" said Rachel, looking at Matt.

"What did I do?" asked Matt.

"Nothing," said Rachel with a now-nothing-can-be-done look.

"Maybe or maybe not, but how do we face them all now?" said Matt.

Just then, Marco said with confidence, "Like always."

"For your knowledge, goblins took our bags, which had the potion and the book to capture them," said Rachel.

"And that's all gone in smoke. So now, how?" said Matt.

"The book," said Marco, "can be any if we wet it with the potion once. As for the potion, we can borrow from Martin and his friends or from the new Hunters." He winked. "And they're not gonna sit idle and test our skills. They too will come to help us as this is their fight too."

"Oh yeah," said Rachel and Matt in unison, and they gave high five to each other and Marco.

Dragoon looked at the burning pile and said, "It seems goblins randomly picked up the Hunters' items, but why didn't they react?"

"There are three to four of those pests," said Dragoon. "They once came into the prison realm but escaped."

"Maybe these goblins might have picked up these Hunters' things unwittingly," said Shenron.

"Anyway," said Dragoon, "this realm's Hunters are in this human city itself, it seems."

"Yes, my brother," said Shenron, "As the goblins didn't go out of the city, they picked these Hunters' stuff from here."

Both brothers laughed wickedly.

None dared to venture out of their houses. The town was in a complete shutdown. Marco was chatting with the others in a group chat in his cell when he said, "Enough, I've had it. I'm gonna reveal myself. Now let those evils stop harassing the innocents."

Before anyone could say anything, Marco packed his bag and walked toward the dragons' lair.

Marco's parents tried to stop him from going out, but they couldn't stop him. They watched him go, and just then, Rachel and Matt arrived in their bikes, followed by Jane's two cars. All of them didn't want Marco to go alone. "Now this must end once and for all," said Jane, getting out from her yellow Audi car.

"Yeah, but not you all alone against them," said Alex.

"Yeah," said Matt and Rachel in unison, "once and for all."

"Now, we against them," said Mike. "We take the fight to them."

Marco's parents watched the small grouping outside their gate, and Marco said, "Okay, Shenron and Dragoon, here comes the Hunters," as they transformed into their Hunter suits.

On seeing and hearing that their son and his friends were the Hunters, they gasped.

Just then, a few goblins walking by spotted them and ran toward them to terrorize and capture them, but then, the twelve were ready to deliver blows by brandishing their swords. Matt's and Rachel's parents and a few people watched from their top room's windows. The kids revealed themselves to be some kind of sword masters. Soon the fight began. Marco and Mike slashed two goblins' chests. Matt and Rachel were almost killed, but Maria took on their attackers, two sturdy-built goblins, from behind. Marco's parents came running outside, but Jane stopped them and said, "You better get Matt's and Rachel's parents and get out of this town. And hurry. We'll explain everything later when we catch up with you." Just then, a goblin leaped, brandishing a pointed stick, but Sasha came in the middle and pushed her sword into the goblin's mouth in midair. The goblin lay dead, stuck with the sword through its mouth. Sasha waved the sword at two other goblins running toward them. The goblin stuck dead to the sword went crashing to the two goblins. The entire neighborhood was looking at the fighting groups. Twelve youths with swords were warring with about fifteen goblins with swords.

Jane shouted, "All of you, get out of Rosewood as fast as you can."

None moved until she shouted again, "The two dragons are coming."

Soon everyone was running helter-skelter to get out of their small town, Rosewood, which had now turned into a battleground.

One of the fighting goblins said, laughing, "How far can they all run? Our masters will terrorize you all, starting with you medley Hunters."

Jane hit the goblin hard and sent its sword flying from his hand to another goblin's mouth. She said, "Who said your foolish masters are coming? Me. And I said it just to see them run to safety." She stabbed the goblin and tossed him into the air with her sword.

Soon the Hunters had destroyed all the goblins except two who ran away in fear toward their masters. By now, most of the townsfolk too were out of Rosewood.

The dragon brothers, who were walking on the streets in their humanoid forms, saw the two injured goblins oozing with green blood come running to them.

"Masters," said one of the injured goblins, "we found the Hunters in Rosewood, but—"

"There are twelve in all, and not three to four as you said," said the other injured goblin.

Just then, the goblin king arrived and said, "These two are low soldiers. Moreover, please give us time, and we'll bring those pests in front of you."

"Then quit boasting and go," roared Dragoon, breathing fire into the road.

The three goblins jumped and ran away in fear.

After a few hours, the goblins appeared in Rosewood. Not a single human was seen outside except twelve teens brandishing swords dripping with green blood. Many goblins lay dead here and there.

"Wow," said Rachel, "just the Hunters and the goblins."

Matt said, slightly laughing, "Good thing the entire neighborhood packed off and left as fast as anything I have seen."

The others too laughed slightly and held their swords tightly in their hands as all the armored goblins came charging. Soon the clash happened. The teens were good, but so were the goblins.

Through the open window of the house beside which he was fighting, Marco picked up a talc powder can from a table and threw it in the air and slashed a cutting blade at it with his sword. The red blade cut the talc can in two and scattered the talc in the air. The smell of the lavender talc distracted everyone, and taking it as a good point, the Hunters stabbed their opponent goblins in their chests and mouths.

Soon all the goblins lay dead after two-hour-long fight. Sasha revolved and slew the goblin king by giving a blow with her sword after Maria kicked him backward.

Just then, Stella spotted a monstrous firefly heading toward the town under the darkening sky, and seated on it was a red-haired gal and the three shining gray ghosts.

"Well," said Stella, "we got company coming."

"Who are they?" said Stella.

"These are some Hunter prisoners—the snake lady, Carolina, three evil ghosts, and their first capture as Hunters in this realm, a monstrous mutant firefly," said Martin.

They all stood brandishing their swords, ready to strike.

Marco said, "Anyone who's got a bit of the potion should apply it on everyone's sword as we have been fighting with these swords for a long time. Just reapply the potion for the effect to stay fresh. Otherwise, we can't fight those pesky ghosts. And, Jane, that firefly killed your dad."

"Well," said Jane, her eyes burning with the fire of revenge, "that firefly is mine."

Maria removed her potion from her car and spilled it on all the swords when they were shown forward.

Matt said, "We gotta capture those ghouls first in some book and then deal with the others."

"Yeah," said Marco, "the potion will help us do that."

Instead of standing to face the oncoming attackers, all twelve scattered.

Marco shouted, "Get into any house, break the doors or windows open. For now, we can adjust, and the owners will understand."

"Okay," shouted Jane and the others in return.

Maria shouted in addition, "If Dragoon and Shenron don't come firing flame attacks."

Matt laughed faintly.

They all ran behind or inside the houses, shattering the windows. Marco asked Maria to pour the potion on the books on each one's hands too just as she had done with the swords.

The attacking members of the dragons' elites split into five to capture the scattered group of Hunters.

As if that wasn't enough, a group of warrior goblins entered the town too. They were shocked to see their dead king's head on the ground along with the dead bodies and body parts of their brethrens scattered here and there.

Jane moved the sword to the sides and then in a circle and unleashed a fiery tornado at the firefly. The firefly was caught in it, and it crashed into a house on the side.

Matt and one of the three ghosts were sneaking around the same house when Matt struck him with his sword and then opened up a book and got down to business.

"Phew!" said Matt. "That was quick."

Sasha, in the meantime, was fighting another ghost, and after striking him with her sword, she jumped out of the house through the window. As the ghost chased her out of the window, he found Sasha opening up a book, smiling wickedly. Two of the five attackers were trapped in two random books they had picked up. Matt had a book on cooking while Sasha had a book on travels. Matt and Sasha spotted each other and laughed and raised their books in the air and showed the books to each other.

Just then, the third ghost charged at Matt, and he flew fast and snatched the book from Matt's hand, but the sword made a slight cut on his arm while he was snatching it and Matt revolved to avoid it. A bit of potion got attached to him. Rising in the air to the height of a tree at the side, the ghost opened the book to have one of his two friends out without thinking about the liquid on his wound. On opening the book, a powerful cyclone-like wind engulfed him and pulled him into the book.

"Nooo . . ." screamed the ghost as he was sucked in.

The book dropped on the lawn. "You shouldn't open it but destroy it to free your friends, foolish ghost," said Matt, mockingly picking up the book.

Just then, Sasha saw a red-haired lady charging at Matt. She was not running on the ground but was levitating a few inches above the ground and charging at him.

But just as she was about to deliver a deadly blow with her poisonous fingernails, Mike stepped in between and took the attack. He crashed into Matt and fell to the ground with the lady having her nails dug into him. Matt went backward a few feet and fell into the children's swimming pool.

Four

$\mathcal{M}$att surfaced fast and saw Mike lying and losing blood while holding Carolina. Carolina was trying to break Mike's tight hold.

At last she broke the tight grip and threw Mike with force into the house on whose ground they were fighting. The windows shattered, and Mike fell inside, bleeding.

"You pesky Hunters," said Carolina and walked toward the pool.

Matt climbed out of the pool on the other side and ran behind the house.

Carolina laughed and began chasing him. When they were behind the house, Matt tripped over a hose, and Carolina ran at him and jumped with her sharp, pointy, and deadly nails dripping with Mike's blood. But the door was kicked open, and Mike jumped in between, brandishing his sword and penetrating it into her chest. "No . . . aaarrrr," screamed the lady in anger and pain.

But before she could regain herself or before Matt could interfere, Mike drew a small protective circle around the lady and unleashed the protective ring spell, holding Carolina and not letting her escape. The lady shrieked with horror as the flames destroyed her to ashes. Mike fell to the ground as Matt ran toward him.

Mike was badly hurt and had lost lots of blood. Others too came running toward them. Jane unleashed three powerful fiery tornados together and destroyed the mutant firefly that was charging at them.

Mike looked at his friends and said, "Well, I'm lucky I met the legends at least," and breathed his last.

"Enough of this," said Stella. "Now let's take the fight to Shenron and Dragoon."

Marco and all of them nodded sadly. They had lost one friend to some realm today. Marco, Maria, Stella, and rest of the gang got into their cars and bikes and sped toward Dragoon and Shenron. On their way, one or two goblins pounced on the bikers, but the bikers had their swords in hand, and they slashed them in midair when they pounced at them.

Dragoon and Shenron were talking, sitting on a bench in their humanoid forms, when a yellow car came at them from behind. The car hit the wooden bench and threw both the humanoid dragons to the ground. The car turned and screeched to a halt.

Both the humanoid dragons stopped in midair after being thrown from the seat.

"You came. We were getting bored," said Dragoon.

"You only four where's the fifth one?" asked Shenron teasingly looking at Steve, Andrews, Stella and Maria making out from their faces Steve was no more.

Maria said, "Yeah, we're eleven, but the twelfth is here with us in our hearts always, and each of our blows to you is from him too." She and the others ran, brandishing their swords at the dragons.

The dragons transformed into their dragon forms and spit fire at the Hunters.

The Hunters avoided it, and they all fired fiery tornadoes except for Matt and Rachel, who slew the goblins who dared to come attacking the Hunters.

"So he died, and now you will too, so don't worry, you'll see him soon maybe. Ha ha ha," said Shenron, laughing. Jane threw a powerful, cutting fiery tornado. The tornado cut Shenron's tail off.

Shenron screamed with pain and anger.

"You scream worse than a girl child," said Stella mockingly.

Jane began to feel dizzy. Matt caught her. He and the others ran with her into a nearby building.

"What happened?" asked Matt.

"The cutting fiery tornado has exhausted her. That is a very powerful offense," said Stella.

"But she unleashed three fiery tornadoes earlier," said Rachel.

"Yeah, but a cutting fiery tornado is ten times more powerful than a fiery tornado. This is one of the most powerful of all the attacks, second only to the destructive ring," said Maria.

"At least Shenron will lose pride. A dragon without a tail is a very rare sight," mocked Jane in her feeble voice.

The others laughed.

Marco and Andrews told all of them to follow them. They reached a room, and through a broken wall, they slid out into the streets at the backside of the building.

They slid out and then quickly got into an opposite building.

Meanwhile, the goblins went inside to bring the Hunters out to their masters. They couldn't find them on the lower floor, and thinking the Hunters were on the next floor, they climbed the stairs, shouting their hunt cry.

The Hunters in the meantime knew that it was time they took a break or they were gonna lose for sure. So they decided to go for now, regroup with their families, and come back with a better plan to defeat the dragons.

They opened a passage to a sewer and crept in and ran.

Matt activated a remote censor to Jane's cars and operated them via GPS. The dragon saw the cars going a little forward. Without thinking about anything, Dragoon flew to the air and fired a powerful fire onto the city below. The fire rained down on the city. Even goblins ran helter-skelter. And then there was a powerful explosion after Shenron rose to the air. The entire city lay in rubbles. Many of the goblins in the city below were vaporized too.

The walls of the sewage were crumbling, and they went into a big pipe as the walls collapsed. The opening was blocked, and they took another route to Winterwood.

The dragons and the rest of the goblins decided that the Hunters died in that explosion.

Meanwhile, the Hunters reached the neighboring town of Winterwood still through the sewage.

After some long walk with no more masks on, they found a manhole lid above. There was a metal ladder to it, and they began climbing.

In Winterwood, everyone was praying for a savior after hearing the big explosion. Just then, they saw the manhole lid in the center of the town being pushed open. They looked in fear, wondering who that was, passing out sticks and steel rods to fight with.

A hand came up and then Matt's head. Behind him was Andrews, followed by Sasha.

Andrews and Matt didn't see the people standing with sticks and metals. But Sasha saw it and shouted, "Aaaaah!"

Rachel, who was climbing out behind them, stood still with her one leg out of the hole.

Just then, Matt's elder brother called out "Matt!" and ran toward him. Others looked. Marco's, Rachel's, and Matt's parents came from the crowd that had formed around them and walked toward them in joy to see them safe.

Matt was relieved that the sticks and metals were not gonna rain on them. Marco later came out.

Jane looked at the surprised people and said, "Let's assemble at the common hall. I think standing here won't be safe."

They all entered the vast town hall of Winterwood.

Jane asked them all to be seated, and they all pushed the chairs one above another into the corner and sat on the floor. Only the Hunters stood.

Jane began, "These dragons come from a parallel universe, and so are all these Hunters except us four," indicating herself, Sasha, Alex, and Martin.

Marco's, Rachel's, and Matt's families looked at their children and then at each other.

"These three," said Michelle, indicating Matt, Marco, and Rachel, "were indeed born here because they had died while coming here from the universe where these four came from"—she indicated Stella, Maria, Steve, and Andrews—"so their energies were sent into this realm, but they are from a totally different universe."

"You mean there's more than one universe?" said an old man.

"Yeah," said Alex.

"That's ridiculous. But honestly, I think you all are from another world, which coincidentally is the same as our Earth," said a man.

Many others said, "Yeah, yeah . . ."

"Then give a better explanation for Shenron, us five, including our late colleague, being here when the portals opened up on one fine day," said Maria coolly.

On hearing her cool lines, they all sat silent, but the man said, "Maybe you all are from some alien world, and you people can travel from one place to another via portals."

"Look," said Stella, "do you people at least agree we're from different worlds?"

They all said, "Hmm . . ."

"Well, believe it or not, there are 126 universes. Each universe is vast. When I say vast, I mean really vast. Otherwise, many questions would have been answered, and someone would have been able to uncover the full secrets by now," said Maria. "And while uncovering, a barrier was opened. This knowledge led to this sort of happening, unfortunately, and thus we're here."

Alex began, "The dragons too live on an Earth in their universe, and they are here to exercise their full strength as they can't do it there peacefully. But their enemies, the Hunters, came here too."

Soon Jane told them about the Hunter legacy, how Rachel, Marco, and Matt are the main players, and how Dragoon and Shenron existed. Everyone listened without interrupting. It seemed as if Jane was a granny telling stories to her grandchildren—all the townsfolk assembled in the hall on one fine Saturday.

Marco and his friends spent the rest of the day joyously with their families without revealing the Hunter suits or weapons that they used when they faced some goblin groups. Even Dragoon, Shenron, and the goblins thought the Hunters were history.

❧

The next day, the entire group of Hunters held a meeting in Marco's temporary house.

"Now what?" asked Stella.

Marco replied, "Sitting here won't do any good as we see the same news daily that the armies are failing."

"So what do you suggest?" asked Rachel.

"Last time we were almost unprepared," said Marco. "We went in rage to make them pay for Mike. But we were foolish to just go at them unprepared."

"We gotta take it one at a time," said Martin, "and make them pay."

"You said it, bro," said Alex, giving a high five to him.

Matt's brother, who was sitting listening to the Hunters, said, "Does this mean you lot are going to face them again?"

"Yeah, dude," said Marco.

"We have to go and stop them once and for all so that you all can roam around freely like before," said Matt.

The brother looked at Matt and smiled, but in his heart, he was saying, *Don't you dare go, dude, but if you go, do come back!*

"It's time," said Matt. "Dragoon, Shenron, and the evil players realize we're back, and this time, they are the history and not us."

Marco and Rachel gave a high five to each other and said in unison, "Oh yeah." Matt and Rachel hugged each other and shared a kiss.

"Wow . . ." said Marco, surprised, "when did this happen?"

Both pulled back, saying sorry.

Marco said, "Come on, you both love each other, so you both hugged the others as friends while you kissed each other. Go, man, you got the hottest girl in MU, buddy." He shoved him toward Rachel.

Matt and Rachel seemed very shy. Matt placed an arm around Rachel's shoulder and stood while Marco smiled happily for his pals, though surprised.

A week passed, and by now, the goblins started terrorizing nearby towns. The army forces rose to combat them, but soon the armies began to fall. Nothing was powerful enough to destroy the dragon siblings.

Soon more major wars broke out. Many of the superpowers got involved, and after a short period, all of America was under the dragon siblings. So were many major countries. The USA, western Asia, and Europe were seen as Dragoon's regime, and South America, Africa, and eastern Asia as Shenron's regime.

Thus three years passed.

The survivors stayed hidden underground. The Hunters made preparations for the attack, and as a start, they fought a group of nasty hobgoblins (yellow-skinned creatures, covered with brown spots and more brutish in their features compared to goblins) to protect a few innocents who were attacked by them.

Five

*M*any years ago, Jordan, Kyle and Marissa, wearing black tights and domino masks, along with the two dragons Shenron and Dragoon in their tall humanoid forms, were fighting a gigantic flying viper which dwarfed even the dragons.

"We shouldn't have destroyed its eggs," said Kyle, "and now it's seriously mad."

"How the heck would we have known that the eggs were below when we fell?" said Shenron.

After a few years, inside a large dark cave, an electric-blue portal opened up.

In humanoid form, the dragons Dragoon and Shenron and the three humans in black tights but with no masks—Kyle, Jordan, and Marissa—looked at it in wonder and at each other and smiled.

"We did it," said Kyle.

"Yeah, let's go in and see where it goes exactly," said Dragoon.

All five walked into the giant portal, smiling and eager to see what was on the other side.

After a few months, Kyle, Jordan, and Marissa were battling Shenron and Dragoon. Shenron was engulfed by strong cyclonic *winds and tried to escape but was caught in a book as Dragoon escaped toward the dark mountains ahead.*

A destructive circle was made, and Shenron was released into it. Shenron roared in pain. Shenron was turned to dust as Jordan, Kyle, and Marissa watched.

Dragoon, hiding behind the thick woods in his humanoid form, watched Shenron dying. He breathed fire into the trees around and transformed into his dragon form and flew away.

Kyle, Jordan, and Marissa saw Dragoon flying away and stared at him and the remains of the destructive circle process.

Once, Queen Akilo battled Dragoon with spells. Jordan, Marissa, and Kyle arrived just in time, distracting Dragoon, and Queen Akilo rolled off the cliff into the lake.

Dragoon again flew off as he saw many of Akilo's forces arrive to aid Marissa, Jordan, and Kyle.

After a few days, in a war between Queen Akilo and Dragoon, Dragoon's three grumpy thin old white-bearded wizards on his back opened up a portal in order to escape defeat, and Dragoon flew in with them on his back before the Hunters could have him captured. Though the book's strong cyclonic winds engulfed them, the portal's pull was powerful, and it sucked Dragoon and his wizards into a new realm.

After some days, the portal opened up, and Dragoon returned. But unknown to him, this time the Hunters and the entire kingdom

were ready to have him killed. He again opened up a portal to return to the other realm and run away. But this time, just before the portal closed, Queen Akilo, Kyle, Jordan, and Marissa ran in front of it and were also sucked into it. The tunnel was very lengthy, filled with turns.

It was a new land. Dragoon had flown away as soon as he was out of the portal. Just then, a few feet ahead, a five-foot-tall young Chinese man stood looking at the dragon flying away with three old men on his back. He was cutting a tree down when this portal appeared and out flew a dragon with three thin white-bearded men on his back, and after three minutes, four humans arrived too—two handsome young men and two beautiful young ladies.

The queen looked around and said, "Dragoon has a beautiful hideout!"

Marissa said, "Yeah, and he might be badly injured to have the portal stay open more than a minute. His mind must have been occupied about getting well, I guess."

"Yeah," said Kyle, "we know Dragoon can be careless when he's in a hurry and scared."

"Yeah," said Jordan, looking at the dumbstruck woodcutter.

In the following minutes, Kyle talked to the woodcutter and learned that he was Ching. And Ching fell in love at first sight with the beautiful, fair-skinned, and long-haired blond, Queen Akilo, when she emerged out of the portal.

In the following days, Ching's kind and caring approach to Queen Akilo had her falling in love with him too.

Days passed, weeks passed, months passed, and at last, Ching married Queen Akilo.

It was a grand celebration in the small village. None knew of Akilo's or her pals' origins, and they believed Ching when he told them he had rescued them after seeing that they had been kicked and led by some soldiers of a neighboring kingdom.

One day, as all were feasting in the hall, Jordan came, pushing the door open and saying, "Fire! Dragoon!"

Just then, two or three village lookout guards came and shouted, "Dragon!"

But the warning was late; the dragon was attacking the village. Jordan, Marissa, Kyle, and Akilo weren't able to do anything.

Jordan said, "We gotta make the potion here to survive."

Kyle nodded.

Ching looked at his friends. While Dragoon was trying to return back to his hideout, his eyes fell on a pregnant woman helping three women to safety. He looked closely, and he thought it was a look-alike of Akilo, but then he saw Jordan, Kyle, and Marissa.

"You followed me here," said Dragoon to himself and roared.

Just then, a portal opened up, and more arrows came toward Dragoon. Their tips had the Hunters' potion applied on them. He flew away up into the sky.

Queen Akilo fell unconscious as her head was hit by a plank that flew at her when a cart exploded. Jordan saw the soldiers from Queen Akilo's universe. One of them saw the queen and Jordan. He went near them. Jordan looked at him and asked just to reconfirm, "Queen Akilo's man?"

The man nodded.

Jordan and that soldier carried the queen into the portal. Jordan thought about getting Akilo to safety and coming back to get his pals. He thought the portal would stay open for a while. Ching, who was separated from his wife, saw that she had been carried into the portal. He, along with Kyle and Marissa, ran toward the portal but were just a few feet away when the portal closed.

"Akilo," shouted Ching, kneeling on the ground as Marissa and Kyle stood behind him. Everything was destroyed. There was fire everywhere. Ching's old father had died, and so were many other villagers.

After a few hours, on Jordan's order, the portal reappeared, and Jordan, along with twelve soldiers, arrived. Ching, Kyle, and Marissa decided to go with Jordan.

After a month or two, Dragoon came back to Akilo's realm. This time, Dragoon had an army of evil goblins and hobgoblins. The attack was sudden. Dragoon's three wizard friends knew how to summon a portal thanks to Dragoon sharing a small bit of power with them to enhance their skills after the friendship of the five had split.

With the help of the portal operator, Hanks, and his promise that he'll open the portal again, Queen Akilo and the Hunters were back on Ching's realm. They hid in a cave. The place where Ching's village and home had stood a few months back was now completely abandoned. Not a soul was in sight. Many houses were destroyed. There were red blood marks here and there.

On the fifth night, as Kyle and Jordan were looking for any sign of Dragoon, they saw a portal opening a few feet ahead, and out came Dragoon and his army.

After many days, another portal appeared. Akilo's parents came this time. On seeing them, Marissa led them to Akilo. With Akilo's parents, they returned back to Akilo's realm.

In the following weeks, there were about five sudden attacks. And this time, Dragoon had men and trolls in his army in addition to the goblins and hobgoblins. Each time, via the secretly created portal below the castle, Akilo would jump forth and back without much thinking that she was vulnerable due to her pregnancy being on the seventh month.

After two more months, Akilo's water burst, and screaming in pain, she gave birth to a beautiful, black-haired, and blue-eyed baby girl in one portal jump.

Akilo said, "While I was in my world, I was just a royal woman, and now within moments, I am back in my hubby's place, I am a royal mom." They all laughed and said congrats.

After two months, the team decided to stop Dragoon's attack. Akilo too was now ready to fight, and they jumped into the portal just before it closed. Dragoon and his army of men and goblins attacked. Some were killed by Akilo, Ching, and the three Hunters. Akilo, with the potion, jumped on Dragoon. Dragoon hit Akilo hard, sending her flying to the portal opening. The army was surprised when they saw their second queen come crashing to the ground. And then out flew the dragon and its three wizard pals, followed by Dragoon's army, the Hunters, and Akilo's husband, Ching. This time, the fight was severe. One of Dragoon's evil men battled powerfully against Akilo and her sword. And before anyone could interrupt, the man dug his sword into Akilo's stomach.

Akilo kneeled on the ground. The man struck his sword into her chest.

Ching, in anger and pain, jumped forth, slashing the head off the man's body.

Ching caught her and laid her head on his lap. Akilo looked at him and said, "Take care of little Jane. I am sorry."

Ching cried out, saying, "No, no!"

Akilo touched Ching's cheek with her bloodied hands and lifted herself a little, still lying, and pulled Ching's face closer and kissed him on the lips. And in the middle of the kiss itself, she breathed her last. She was gone.

Meanwhile, Dragoon decided to pull back, and his portal casters opened a portal after getting a slash from a knight's poison-dipped spear. Marissa, Jordan, Kyle, and Ching saw them escaping and, brandishing their swords, ran at them in anger, slashing everything in their path. Dragoon and his portal casters jumped in. By this time, Marissa, Kyle, Jordan, and Ching jumped in too after jumping over dead bodies of two falling trolls that had faced some of Akilo's men.

Inside the portal, it was four against four. But the sorcerers were powerful, and they unleashed a powerful electric attack. Marissa, Jordan, and Kyle were hit badly. Ching was hit minutely as Kyle pushed Ching to the ground, and so Ching fell unconscious. Before the dragon could unleash a deadly fire, the portal opened, casting them into the lake below. The dragon beat his wings faster and prevented himself from hitting the water. He caught his three men with his neck, tail, and back, and he flew off as Marissa, Jordan, Kyle, and Ching fell unconscious and hit the cold water. Ching regained his senses and found his three friends drowning along with him. He swam toward them and pulled them to shore. At shore, they didn't move a finger. Ching knew that he had lost them too. He shouted, "Nnnnnooooo!"

After eighteen years, Ching, in the meantime, created a team called Hunters in honor of the three friends.

Ching and Akilo's daughter had by now become a very beautiful young girl. Once, she and three other Hunters attacked a gargoyle. All four were just novices. And for their bad luck, the gargoyle was powerful and turned them to stone before Ching could arrive.

After almost a century, Ching spotted the three evil wizards. He followed them in the dark shadows of the trees and saw his main foe, Dragoon. He was just about to attack and make them pay for his losses when he heard one of them say, "The Hunters are dead, and even if they return, they can't challenge us or you as we have become powerful over the many years that had passed."

Ching thought, My friends' return!

Dragoon said, "Hmm, it's been 100 years. Who will remind them of their past now?"

"My lord," said one of them, "their friend, that Ching, had been recruiting new Hunters. He must be too old now, he'll breathe *his last soon. And speaking of the other three, as they are dead, their spirits will be thrown out into this realm, and it might take some time for their spirits to regain full power and be born again. Before that, even we should go back as it's been too long since that Akilo's death."*

Ching fumed with anger and jumped out from behind the huge rock and said, "That's Queen Akilo for you, wretched ones."

Ching was fast, and his sudden attack was totally unpredicted. He slashed the three men's heads off their bodies. Dragoon swept his tail. Ching jumped over it, slashing it and delivering a cut.

"My wife, Akilo, had given me powers to live longer, just like your three evil sorcerers. And now I'll find my friends when they are reborn, and till then"—he opened a blank book—"you'll stay here."

Dragoon was engulfed by a strong wind, and he was pulled into it.

"You'll die in the hands of our mutual pals, Dragoon," said Ching, looking at the book and shutting it.

The news of the Hunters spread like wildfire after three years. But the dragons proved themselves to be too strong to be defeated after the Hunters hid.

The dragons were ruling, and none were able to stop them. Many tried but failed. Three years had passed since the dragons started ruling. The Hunters, along with some people, stayed hidden, surviving attacks. At last, the Hunters had had enough.

"Now," said Marco, "we have to fight."

"We did not become Hunters just to hide in fear but to destroy the ones unleashing these fears," said Marco.

They decided to destroy Dragoon first and then Shenron.

Dragoon had positioned himself in and around the White House in his humanoid and dragon forms. The White House lay in ruins. Half of the construction was destroyed by fire. The Washington Monument's upper half was gone—to be precise, destroyed. The Hunters got two terrain rovers and rode them to Washington. Sasha, Marco, Rachel, Matt, Alex, and Jim, a short blond-haired, well-built man were in one while Maria, Jane, Stella, Martin, Steve, Andrews, and Dave, a bald, well-built man were in another. Both Jim and Dave were United States's young soldiers who had just taken their exams and were waiting to be called for the country's defense.

The rovers headed straight for the White House. Few goblins stood in the path to stop them, but the rovers just went ahead and crushed them to death. Heavy blades were stuck to the rims of the tires, and few globins and hobgoblins that moved from getting rammed by the rovers' front were cut to death by these blades. Few goblins and hobgoblins closed the gate and stood behind it as the rovers came forward. Instead of slowing down, both the rovers accelerated. They crashed into the gates, disconnecting the gates from the walls and sending them flying at the evil party that stood a little back and killing the hobgoblins and goblins that came in their path. One was trying to use a rocket launcher, but Alex fired a bazooka very fast at it, killing it and a few near it. On hearing the noises, Dragoon came out. He was in his seven-foot-tall red humanoid form, wearing a yellow cloth around his waist, and on seeing the arriving Hunters and killing a goblin in their way, he breathed fire, looking up in anger.

"This time we are gonna end you once and for all, dear Dragoon," said Stella mockingly to Dragoon as she clicked a button on her wristband.

"Please work," she said in a low tone to the band while clicking the button, shutting her eyes tightly and praying in her heart.

Suddenly some kind of mercury liquid shot out from her wristband and engulfed her, and then it materialized around her, turning her into an opaque giant steel lady. She kept on growing and at last halted when she was about fifteen feet tall with dark eyes and a long thin, slender ninja blade attached to her waist.

"Cool," said Andrews.

Dragoon transformed into his ferocious dragon form. Stella ran, brandishing her sword. Dragoon ran forward too when Stella jumped and caught Dragoon's long neck while landing. She pulled the neck and flipped the dragon, sending him crashing into a group of goblins hiding behind some big rubble to attack the Hunters.

"Wow," said Matt.

"Good thing she brought it," said Steve.

"You mean she had it all this time with her?" said Rachel.

"Yeah, and even I have one," said Steve.

"Then why didn't you both use it even once before?" asked Marco furiously.

"Till now, even we didn't know it had started working," said Steve. "We have been trying ever since we came into your realm, but due to some magnetic disruption when we crossed through the portal, these bands were disrupted, and they had been dead so far. But now, all of a sudden, they're working. Even two nights before, when we tried it in Winterwood, we didn't get any useful results.

"These two have the latest models that were created just a day before we arrived here, but they had never been used before so we don't know their pros and cons," said Andrews. "They take on the physique of the user and an android. Stella's takes a girl's form, and his, a man's form." He looked at Steve.

"So, Steve," said Rachel, "I guess it's time you entered the battle zone as we don't have much chance when we have a fifteen-footer fighting alone with an eighty-foot dragon. After these long years, who knows how strong he is now? After all, this isn't like being in a book."

"You're right. That is Hunter 001, and mine is Hunter 002," said Steve, and he ran toward Dragoon, who had just swept his tail and sent Stella crashing into the White House. Steve activated his band, hoping it would work in time. He shut his eyes tightly, hoping, as he jumped at Dragoon from a piece of rubble near Dragoon. Mercury liquid emerged from the band and engulfed him, and soon he was a sixteen-foot steel-armored human-like warrior with dark eyes and a long thin, slender ninja blade attached to his waist. He caught Dragoon's neck by surprise and flipped him into the lawn.

"Wow . . ." Jane laughed. "That's the second time within fifteen minutes that the mighty Dragoon was tossed."

The others laughed too.

Dave and Jim fired rocket launchers at a group of hobgoblins and had them flying into the air.

Dragoon was surprised to see the new technology of the Hunters. He saw the sixteen-foot-tall warrior standing his ground firmly and the fifteen-foot-tall warrior whom he had sent crashing into the White House now emerging out of the ruined building.

Dragoon took to the air and looked down at both of his giant foes and said, "Do you meddling Hunters think you can defeat me with your new toys?"

Steve said, "Yeah, we're looking forward to that."

Stella said, "And we are happy that you got hard times now, you freaky lizard."

Dragoon had enough and came at both of them. He crashed to them and sent them crashing into the White House. Dragoon transformed into his humanoid form but stood eighteen feet tall with his spiky tail.

Blows were delivered here and there. Steve and Stella were hitting Dragoon furiously, and Dragoon was hitting them back hard. With each blow, it seemed as if thunders were rolling. On Dave and Jim's orders, many rebels too reached Washington, and now humans were fighting the goblins and hobgoblins.

Marco looked at Matt and Rachel. Andrews and Maria saw them looking at each other, and then as if they were connected telepathically, Matt ran toward the rover and took out a book and a flask with some potions.

They understood what the trio was thinking now. They looked at each other and nodded.

Just then, Stella came out crashing through an intact wall. They looked at Stella, who pointed at them. But when she pointed, a powerful laser blast was fired from her shoulder. Andrews and Maria jumped out of the way. The laser beam hit ten warrior goblins that were gonna sneak an attack on Maria and Andrews. Stella looked at her shoulder and said, "Wow, we got laser blasts too. I was just pointing out."

Stella said to herself, "Self note 1: gotta learn the attacks clearly after this fight, or we may harm the civilians."

"Yeah, you just knew that now?" asked Matt, confused.

"You lot are using that armor for the first time. Now, I see," said Rachel, laughing.

Marco interrupted the talks and said, "Look, Steve is fighting now and is keeping him busy."

"Hmm," said the others.

"You get the potion on Dragoon via any cuts, and then we'll capture him in a book, and we can put an end to this fight," said Marco.

Stella nodded and took the conical flask from Marco and ran back into the White House.

Matt took the book and ran behind her, followed by Jane, Rachel, Marco, Maria, and Andrews.

Inside, the fight was furious. Dragoon kicked and sent Steve crashing to the stairs. Before he could deliver a killing stroke, Stella kicked Dragoon hard and sent him crashing through the walls. Stella then jumped with her sword and delivered a blow on his neck but missed as he jumped out of its path, and the long slender sword could just make a cut on his tail with which he tried to hit Stella. Dragoon howled with pain but managed a smile and said, "You missed me, darling."

"Oh no, I didn't, darling," said Stella, throwing the potion on Dragoon's wound. The wound got drenched with potion, and then it happened before Dragoon knew. Matt opened the book. Dragoon felt air howling around him, and he was sucked into the book.

Dragoon's sketch formed on three pages—two of which featured chicken, and one, a broccoli dish.

"Well now, he will be an expert in making broccoli and chicken dishes, I hope," said Matt as the others laughed.

Steve and Stella transformed back into their normal forms. They first shrunk to their normal size, then the mercury armors split up into small columns of droplets and went back into the bracelets.

"End of one," said Jim, giving Dave a high five.

"Now, mission Shenron," said Marco as all geared up for the next fight.

The news of Dragoon's defeat spread faster than wildfire. Shenron was shocked to hear it. He decided to do a hibernating type of disguise to increase his strength manyfold. He was happy he had learned that technique well in the previous realm before he came to this one. He rose to the air and disappeared for a month while the Hunters hunted him fruitlessly. They arrived in China too in hopes of finding some trace, but nope, there was none. The people throughout the world continued to live their lives with no dragons around. One was gone, and the other, everyone thought to be hiding in fear after his brother's defeat.

One day the Hunters decided to just visit the Himalayas after hearing about the monks there. They started to trek. Shenron seemed to be gone, so the Hunters couldn't do anything else till they get some clues. But things were destined to change.

While trekking a mountain, they spotted an old monastery in the mountains. The monastery's roof had a long brown dragon coiled on it. They took it as the ancient monastery's design and were about to go on with their trek when Alex said, "That's odd. How come we're not seeing any soul around? And the dragon coiling the temple seems to be missing its damn tail."

"Maybe they're inside busy with something, and maybe the design was made only halfway and then left alone," said Martin.

Just then, two of the cemented eyes snapped open, then suddenly, the ceiling collapsed, and the whole dragon design on the roof came to life and took to the air. It came down at the Hunters very fast.

The Hunters were taken by surprise, and they just ducked out of the way of the dragon's deadly claws. The dragon landed near them, and its skin began to change to reddish green from cement brown. The dragon looked bigger and stronger than before.

Shenron transformed into his humanoid form, but his humanoid form was missing the tail. He said, "I was waiting for today for a long time."

"Where are the people?" said Alex.

"And how's your tail?" said Jane mockingly.

The dragon glared furiously.

Rachel looked at Jane and said, "Even though he is a menace, don't mock his feelings. At least, we can't go as low as this menace."

"Sorry," said Jane.

Rachel just smiled in return, and Shenron said, "Enough of your talks, and now I'll make you pay for my loss. Some of these monks made pleasant meals." Shenron licked his lips and continued, pointing his finger to a few bald monks coming out with swords and axes, "And the rest, here they come. Now soon, let's see how the Hunters taste."

"Well, I take back my words," said Rachel, looking at Jane and winking.

Jane said mockingly, "I too take back my apology. Hope your bloody tail is waiting for you before you pass off into some other universe."

Shenron fumed with anger and commanded his troops to kill them all.

Maria looked at their faces and saw that their eyes' pupils were dim and gray. Preparing herself to fight, she said, "This monster has brainwashed and corrupted them, and now they stand for him."

The monks surrounded the Hunters and walked toward them, brandishing their tools.

"Please move aside," said Rachel. "We mean you no harm."

They were still moving closer.

"That filthy reptile has all of them under his command," said Andrews, "so no use."

The circle closed, and soon the Hunters were kicking the monks. Few fell off the edge and hit the slope and went tumbling down to the next flat surface, few went on, and few went tumbling to their deaths.

Jane took out a stunner and stunned the remaining ones, and they fell unconscious. Shenron grew in size, and just then, Steve activated his wristband. Stella too did the same, and soon both were engulfed with mercury and transformed into fifteen—and sixteen-foot human-like warriors.

Shenron was taken aback like his brother as he had never calculated this kind of change when dealing with the Hunters. Shenron was a humanoid about twenty feet tall, reddish, with a green cloth, and was taller than Dragoon's humanoid form.

"So you got tricks up your sleeves," said Shenron, trying not to look surprised.

"Unfortunately," said Steve, "you are about to feel them."

"When we say *feel*," said Stella, "we mean *f-e-e-l, feel,* just like your brother did."

Now on hearing this, Shenron's face began to lose the confidence he earlier felt in him.

Both ran toward him, and Steve was quick. He ran, jumped, and landed on the ground two feet away from Shenron and delivered a hard punch on Shenron's nose. Shenron was taken aback and went a bit backward.

Shenron quickly regained himself and was about to deliver Steve a hard punch when Stella did a somersault and delivered a kick on his face.

Shenron fell sideways.

These tiny ones are indeed tiny, but they pack a punch, thought Shenron, getting up and rubbing his cheek. He transformed into his dragon form. Both the Hunters came running at him, and with his neck, he just swept them off their feet, off the cliff, and into the trees below.

Then he noticed the rest of the Hunters running toward him, clutching their swords. But before he could breathe fire and destroy them, or at least try, Stella and Steve were in the air and landed in the middle.

"That was quick," said Matt with admiration.

Just then, both Steve and Stella's techs started to fuse, and before Shenron stood a new gray ninja robot. And it was about three to four feet taller than the solo versions. Both Hunter 001 and Hunter 002 have fused. It was now controlled by Stella and Steve. It looked too equipped for the fight too, and it was brandishing two fiery, aura-emitting broad, long ninja blades. It looked like a giant steel-armored ninja similar a bit to Steve's. This one had two black lines below its dark eyes which come to a halt two inches from the mouth.

The new Hunter toy had metallic skin that looked like liquid metal. Not even a single nut or bolt on a connecting part was visible, but it had a single connective metallic skin.

"Wow!" said Marco and Matt, looking at each other with amazement and surprised joy. "This time we got more tricks up our sleeves."

"Hot!" Rachel said, whistling. Jane too whistled.

Shenron transformed into his near-human form, which was twenty feet tall, and came at the new Hunter tech, but the new tech was faster than even Shenron could assume. It ducked his blow and hit him on the face hard, sending him rolling off the cliff.

"Meet Hunter 003," said Steve.

Shenron transformed into his dragon form and, in anger, rose to the air, tearing a few trees apart. Marco, meantime, threw a conical flask at the new Hunter tech. Shenron was a bit hurt and was bleeding in the face when the giant Hunter tech caught the flask and threw it directly on Shenron's face. The flask came at his face. It shattered on hitting his face, causing a few injuries, and the liquid wet his face. Shenron understood what the liquid was and flew away to avoid capture, but the Hunters were quick. They had the book out of the bag and opened it.

Shenron tried to fly away, but a force like that of a tornado engulfed him and pulled him into the book. On the very next three pages after Dragoon's pic, Shenron's sketch was formed on the pages of two other chicken dishes and a prawn dish.

Marco unleashed the destructive circle, and then it was very fast. Dragoon and Shenron were released into the fiery circle, and the dragons roared in pain and got destroyed. Before a final white light engulfed them, Marco, Matt, and Rachel winked at the dragons.

"Why did you do this?" asked Andrews.

"Coz this is our home for now," said Marco, looking at Matt and Rachel, who nodded in agreement. All were looking at the three Hunters.

Meanwhile, somewhere in the midst of a city, a pitch-black serpent-like dragon with bits of yellow here and there on its body appeared out of nowhere and roared with green fire coming out of its mouth. Everyone ran, scared.

"Now, Flireon is back," said the black dragon, breathing fire into the sky.

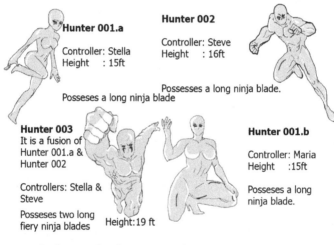

Hunter 001.a

Controller: Stella
Height   : 15ft

Posseses a long ninja blade

Hunter 002

Controller: Steve
Height   : 16ft

Posseses a long ninja blade.

Hunter 003
It is a fusion of
Hunter 001.a &
Hunter 002

Controllers: Stella &
Steve

Posseses two long
fiery ninja blades

Height: 19 ft

Hunter 001.b

Controller: Maria
Height   :15ft

Posseses a long
ninja blade.

Reference sketches just to enhance your imagination

Six

*M*any *centuries ago, in some other realm or universe among the 126 realms or universes scattered, three dragons in humanoid forms were fighting fiercely as Marissa, Kyle, and Jordan were climbing up the cliff. Dragoon, in his twenty-foot red near-human form with a yellow cloth tied around his waist, and Shenron, in his twenty-foot near-human form identical to Dragoon's form with a green cloth around his waist, were fighting with Flireon in his twenty-foot blackish-yellow near-human form wearing a yellow cloth tied around his waist and spiky tail. Out of nowhere, Kyle, Jordan, and Marissa appeared and distracted him, and Dragoon and Shenron spit out at Flireon a deadly magical liquid mixed with their flames, which had him shine with pain and break into tiny dust.*

"Wow," said Marissa, "you destroyed our last powerful common foe."

"No!" said Shenron, "He's not destroyed yet. When—if— me and Dragoon die, he'll be freed."

"Freed!" said Kyle, Jordan, and Marissa in unison.

"Yeah, which is never gonna happen," said Dragoon. "We mixed the fire with the magical liquid, and so he's not dead fully, but now his energies are split within this realm itself and will reconnect to recreate him only after our death coz it's been linked with us as we drank it to spit it along with our fire."

"Now that's like more than a billion years. And by then, even our world will be too advanced for him to threaten, and he will be primitive then," said Marissa, "as you dragons have very long lives and you both are siblings and not foes."

"Not just us," said Dragoon. "Even you three are powerfully clever. Luckily, we're pals and are on the same side."

All five laughed. Dragoon and Shenron transformed from their humanoid forms back to their dragon forms. Kyle and Marissa got on Shenron while Jordan got on Dragoon, and off they went.

For three years, Earth was ruled by the dragons, and now, after long fights, the dragons were gone forever. A month back, the Hunters had destroyed them. The Hunters were sitting with some people under the moonlight, then Andrews said, "Tomorrow I guess the portals might be here, and we'll be back in our universe."

Sasha asked, "How can you be sure?"

"Look, our people know we are not dead," said Maria, clicking a button on her wristband. "If we had died, they would have known it as the computer over there denotes us as alive with a blue dot and if we die, it becomes a red dot. And now they will know that the work is done when the dots turn from blue to green, and if we send out a signal that shows yellow instead of green, then that means we are trapped. It's dark yellow if we are in the middle of a mission, and pale yellow if the mission's ended but we are trapped."

Others too pressed the third button on their respective wristbands just as Jordan and Marissa, "What did you lot just do?"

"We clicked the Hunter tracking beacon of our realm," said Andrews.

Steve began, "In our realms, when Hunters reach the end or get trapped somewhere before or after their mission, they click this beacon on their wristband, and this will send a signal to the headquarters, pinpointing the current location, so now the others will be here to take us back home."

"We understood about the signal being sent to pick up comrades," said Matt, "but how can the signal travel to a computer in a different universe, and after how many days would they receive it after you have sent it?"

Stella said, "Every universe has small, minute gaps all over, and thus this signal travels at a greater speed than light through these gaps and reaches almost every universe, and luckily, thanks to the details that your earlier forms— Marissa, Jordan, and Kyle—gave for its construction, the center pinpoints it. It takes two days to one week."

"Physics!" said Marco, looking at Rachel and Matt.

"Has this worked before too?" asked a young teenage boy who was sitting with them and listening very attentively.

"Yeah!" said Andrews. "When once we went after another universe-jumper psycho a few years ago before we came here."

"That time you went to another universe or realm?" asked Matt.

"Yeah," said Andrews, "but we didn't meet any lookalike or anyone we know. Maybe they were somewhere else or maybe they didn't exist then, same as here."

The boy said, "Cool. I too wanna travel places and destroy the evil scums. I'll be a Hunter too. When's the next recruitment day?"

Marco replied, "Not soon, ha ha ha. You just go and save the people around you and yourself, and when it's time, you'll be one."

"Hmm," said Steve, amazed.

All dispersed back into their destroyed homes and slept.

∽

After two days, by mid noon, an electric-blue portal opened up in the park and out came two heavily armored soldiers. They clicked a button on their respective wristbands, and their helmets faded off. One was a sturdy red-haired man while the other was a blond guy.

"So you're here," said Maria.

The red-haired man said, "Yes, ma'am—" and stopped in mid-sentence on seeing Rachel with Maria. "Marissa!" said both men in amazement.

Just then, Marco and Matt arrived, and on seeing them, the two newcomers exclaimed, "Kyle and Jordan."

"Let me explain," said Stella, and she told them everything. The two newcomers looked at the trio and Jane in amazement. They even bowed to Jane in respect as she's a princess in their realm as her origin claims.

"So you guys not coming?" asked Steve.

"Hmm . . . Not now. Let's first settle everything as its just back to normality," said Marco, winking.

The portal stayed open the entire time, and then Steve and the others bid them farewell. And they went into the portal, and the portal closed.

Meanwhile somewhere else, Flireon terrorized the lands one after another, and soon in two years, that universe's Earth was under Flireon. None knew what to do. Flireon had long been gone from that realm thanks to five amateurs—two dragons, Dragoon and Shenron, and their three human pals—and their lives had flourished well, but then now he was back and was terrorizing every soul. The Hunter clan was never ever formed here, and thus all were rather unprepared for the return of Flireon. Flireon destroyed to pieces the giant statues of his five amateur enemies in the central town, and everyone ran in fear.

Two years had passed since the other realm's Hunters departed. Sitting in a pub, Matt, in a blue checked shirt, said, "Well, we started with a firefly five years ago and went up to an army of goblins and trolls, and the genetic hybrid two hours ago. Well, we were lucky each time."

"Yeah," said Marco, "after Carolina's and Dragoon's attacks, we learned never to keep them in a book itself coz they could get lucky."

"Yeah," said Rachel, "and we'd have to pay a hefty price."

Just then, a classmate, a short brown-haired man, Max, came and sat next to Marco and said, "I wanted to ask many times, but I forget each time. Those three ghosts said once that you three caught them first in our school."

"Hmm . . ." The trio nodded.

"Then how come," said Max, "none of the school remember such an incident? Neither did I hear anyone speak of this."

"Actually," said Marco, "what you heard is true, but after the incident, to keep our identities a secret, we released a liquid in our hand which destroys the memory of anything that occurred in the last one hour, and so many of you couldn't recollect what happened a few hours then, and so even that boy couldn't figure out how he reached on the pole when he was lucky to zoom past the pole when one of the ghosts threw him out to death."

"And that foolish ghosts didn't bother to clarify whether he died or not, so he was really *l–u–c–k–y*," said Matt.

"But," said Rachel, "thanks to Shenron and Dragoon's rule, many know our identities now."

"Hmm," said the others.

Jane said, "We could have asked them to give info and could have a portal constructed, and we could visit them. I miss those Hunters."

Just then, a portal opened up in the middle of the pub.

All were amazed and waited to see who would come through. But the portal closed as quickly as it had opened. No one came out.

Meanwhile in another universe,

A short-haired brunette came running to the canteen where many were sitting, sipping coffee, and talking.

"A portal opened up," she said, heaving.

All were amazed. Stella said, "How could that be?"

"Where?" asked a slightly fat, white-haired, elderly man.

"In . . ." said the new girl, still heaving, "Gloria's Flower and Antique Shop."

Steve said, "What! At Gloria's? That's strange. And moreover, all unregistered ones are destroyed while the registered ones are in our command and custody."

"Looks like someone has made it," said the fat, white-haired, elderly man.

All looked at each other, wondering who it could be and that too in a public shop.

Two days passed after the sudden appearance of a portal in the middle of the pub. Jane was skiing downhill. She was racing with Martin. She was leading when Martin shouted, "So what's your plan?"

"No plan," said Jane, shouting back. "Tomorrow we will return back to New Winterwood and then—"

Just then, a few feet to the right, a portal opened up again. Jane lost her balance and fell face first to the snow as Martin stopped next to her. The portal closed again as suddenly as it had appeared.

Both looked at each other in amazement.

Meanwhile, in another realm, a portal opened in the middle of the city and then closed. Luckily, none were hurt, but this time, unlike last time, there were strong winds, and two to three small stalls nearby were ripped off from the grounds. The entire worldwide Portal Authorizing Centre (PAC) went nuts as when they checked the first area, a second portal opened up about 3,000 miles away.

"So," said the elderly man at PAC., "we got more than one outburst here from two different places that are miles apart from each other."

"You mean," said Andrews, interrupting, "we have to find two illegal portal constructs now instead of one?"

"Yeah," said the elderly man, Dave. "The constructs are at least as big as a one-and-a-half-storey building, and none can transport them across check posts in two days without catching PAC's attention."

Everyone in the room looked at each other in wonder, then Steve said, "Unless these ones are one and the same, and someone made them small and easy for transport."

All looked at him in wonder and thought, what if he was right?

In the Realm 115, Martin and Jane told Alex and Michelle about the appearance of the portal.

Sasha seemed to be in deep thought, pouring down her throat cold water from a cold bottle from the fridge of the inn's cafe. Alex looked at her pouring the cold water and said, "Here we're drinking hot coffee in this cold place to keep ourselves from freezing over, and here you're drinking cold water directly from the fridge. Weirdo."

Sasha mocked him by showing her teeth, "Heee . . . I love cold, and this cold can't affect me after being brought up in the north unlike you guys."

She then picked up a serious tone and said, "Jane, you're a daughter of two universes, and you said that your mother gave birth to you during one of her portal travels."

"Where're you getting to?" asked Alex.

Michelle placed a finger on her lips, indicating Alex and the other two to be silent and said, "You also said that you have heard your father say once that this portal travel can cause some kind of minute change in the DNA of the traveler."

"Hmm . . . Yeah," said Jane.

Michelle again placed her finger on her lips, indicating silence, and said, "What if your parents' portal travel affected you when you were about to be born, and what if it's you who's opened the portals?"

"What!" said Alex, Martin, and Jane in unison, surprised.

"Look, both the times these portals appeared, you were there," said Michelle.

"So was Martin," said Alex.

"He's a gone case, so leave him out," said Michelle teasingly.

Martin looked as if he wanted to argue, but he knew it was no use arguing with Sasha. She'll argue till the other admits they were wrong even if they were right. She's good . . . too good. And too much time will be lost in the silly argument when there are things to be cleared up.

"Look, dear," said Michelle to Jane, "you have a history with portals, and what if the portals affected you when you were a sweet teeny-weeny baby in your mother's womb? Well, dear, just think of opening one just down that cliff." Michelle pointed at a cliff through the window on the other side of their inn.

Jane said, "Well, here goes nothing." She thought, but nothing happened.

Martin mocked Sasha, "So much for your theory. Look, there's a portal." He gestured his palm at the same cliff.

Suddenly a portal appeared.

Martin was taken aback, and so were the others. He fell backward in his chair, and everyone in the pub looked at him.

"Lost my balance!" said Martin, getting up.

All resumed their work.

"How the heck did that happen?" said Martin and again tried the hand movement, but nothing happened.

Jane thought, and a portal opened up in the cafe itself. Sasha was looking at Jane the entire time.

"I didn't do that," said Martin.

Then Sasha said, "She did it."

All looked at Jane.

Jane said, "Me?"

"Yeah, you" said Sasha, "Earlier you thought about creating a portal and they appeared, but they only appeared a few minutes after you thought of creating them. The same thing happened on that cliff too." She pointed to the cliff and asked, "Now you were thinking of having one here, weren't you?"

Jane said, "Yeah, I was just trying what you said."

"But—" Alex said.

"No," Sasha said mockingly and laughed. "Marty was just a coincidence as he is most of the time."

"He just teased my theory as usual, but then the portal appeared a bit slowly, and so we thought it was Marty," said Sasha.

Martin said, "So Jane can indeed open a doorway to other universes. Terrifically awesome."

Meanwhile, in some other realm, the portals appeared and closed in a swampy forest, then in the middle of the gathering of some heinous demons in some deserted rocky plain, and after a few minutes, another one opened up in the middle of an ancient knight statue, destroying it to pieces.

The next day, in Jane's new house in the new town called New Winterwood, Rachel, Matt, and Marco joined the gang when Alex, Sasha, and Martin told them everything. Jane stood up and pointed at the empty noon road from her window and said, "Let's see."

After a few seconds, a portal opened up, and when Jane thought it to close, it closed.

"Wow," said Matt, "you can open and close a doorway whenever you want."

"Why didn't this sort of thing happen earlier?" asked Rachel.

"Because she too, just like us, never thought about the possibilities of another universe, and maybe she wasn't too stressed like now."

"Stress?" said Matt.

"Yeah," said Sasha, winking, "she missed her new friends, *and* she has fallen for one of our new pals."

"What!" said Jane, blushing.

"Who is it, my dear?" said Marco teasingly.

In another realm again, the portal opened up for two minutes in an abandoned, half-destroyed house a few feet away from the location of the very first, sudden portal.

All in the PAC were now confused. They had even thoroughly searched the area for the last few days till an hour ago but couldn't find a clue.

"But to which universe does it open up to?" asked Marco.

"I guess maybe our new friends' universe, coz she has a tie with that universe. And she misses someone of that universe more," mocked Sasha.

"Next time, let's find it out," said Rachel.

"But how?" asked Alex.

"Let's throw a camcorder the next time she summons one and pull it back before she closes it, and let's see what image we get," said Rachel.

"She can open them for as long she wants, I guess," said Rachel, "from the sudden on and off to one that stayed open now for about two minutes."

"Hmm." Everyone nodded.

And then after two hours, they all decided to go ahead with Rachel's idea. This time Jane summoned a portal in the middle of the house's hall, and they threw in a camcorder with a rope tied to its straps.

Meanwhile, in PAC's universe, Dave, Maria, Stella, Steve, and Andrews were standing near the latest portal's spot when another portal opened up just across the road and a camcorder came out flying. They ran toward it. The camcorder was pulled back toward the portal, but its rope got entwined in a thorny bush and broke off, and after a few seconds, the portal closed.

All five reached the bush and picked up the camcorder. Two labels were stuck on it with the name M^2.

Andrews and the others looked at each other and said, "No way!"

"Our cam!" said Martin.

"Something caught it," said Alex, holding the other end of the broken rope they had tied to the camcorder to pull it back.

Jane hit Alex on the head and said, "You idiot, that was a new one."

Alex rubbed his head and said, "Who told you to come up with weird *ideas*?"

Rachel and Marco held their laughter; just then, Jane fainted.

"Seems she can't summon more than one portal for a start now," said Alex, carrying her to the sofa.

Looking through the camcorder's records, the four gazed at the big central computer screen. The camcorder was connected to the central computer. One pic showed Jane, Alex, Martin, and Michelle, and then there were pics of Rachel, Marco and Matt. The elderly man said, "Marissa, Jordan, and Kyle."

There were many pics and videos.

A few years before, Martin was taking some pics of Sasha under the moonlit sky. After taking some pics, they were about to return when they spotted two shadows under the red oak tree on a small hillock. When the moonlight fell on the two shadows, Martin and Sasha saw that, it was Jane and Andrews. Both were slowly kissing each other.

"Now that's a special moment," said Martin and clicked a snap.

The kissers felt the sudden flash, but Martin had captured the kiss in his camera.

The kissing couple's pic was shown on the screen. Andrews blushed.

"Dude," said Stella, "you hid it."

"Who is she?" asked Dave as many turned to look at Andrews.

"She's Jane, the pal of the other realm's Hunters and also Queen Akilo's daughter, Princess Jane of the Shen-vom Dynasty," said Steve.

"Queen Akilo!" said many in amazement.

Maria began, "Yeah, that's a bit of a complicated story, and please be seated."

"Why didn't you report about them to me before?" questioned Dave sternly.

"We did, sir," said Steve.

"Yeah, you lot just said you were helped by some Hunters on that realm and nothing else," said Dave sternly again.

"Jane herself had told me that we shouldn't tell unless they were ready," said Andrews.

Maria then told them about Jane's origin and her life as a Hunter.

After listening, all were speechless.

"Now what?" said Dave.

"We wait and know how they are connected with these portals' appearances at least one to two times more coz as far as I know, they don't possess any technology to open a portal," said Stella.

All nodded or said, "Hmm . . ." Dave watched the screen showing a snap of the two realm's Hunters smiling and posing together with Jane.

♋

Marco said, "I have heard that love can happen all of a sudden, but can die peacefully if the love is let go. But still, falling in love is absurd, I guess."

"At least because of that absurdness, we discovered a new power that our Hunter group has," said Rachel. "We created the clan, and now we have a live, walking portal manipulator among us."

Matt said, "Cool. We rock."

All laughed.

Marco said, "I have a camcorder at home. I'll get it, and we shall put that in and see where this opens up tomorrow."

All agreed, and the trio left for their homes.

The next day, they all met in one of the five parks of New Winterwood. And this time, Marco was ready with the camcorder. He had already tied a strong elastic rope to one end of the straps. The previous camcorder had a normal rope, but this one was tied with strong elastic rope. When others saw the rope tied, he said, "I'm not gonna lose this. If I do, my big bro's gonna kill me."

"Is it his?" asked Rachel.

"Yeah, it's his," said Marco. "Our uncle Philips presented it to him when he won a trekking competition in a camp he went to some years back. Heee . . ."

A few minutes after moving to a side area near the forest, Jane summoned a portal. All crossed their fingers, and Marco threw in his camcorder.

Meantime, in the other realm, a giant monster was attacking the city. The portal opened up next to the monster in the centre of the city. On seeing the camcorder coming and hitting it on the head, it caught the camcorder and pulled it, and then out of the portal came Marco, Matt, Rachel, Jane, and Sasha, one after the other.

Meanwhile, in the other universe, everything happened very quickly. Something pulled the rope. Marco fell forward and got pulled into the portal. Matt jumped and caught his legs, but both were pulled in. Rachel and Jane jumped and caught each of Matt's legs, and Sasha jumped and caught Jane's legs. But the pull from the other side was strong, and all were pulled into the portal. Before the others could catch them, the portal closed.

Now in one corner adjacent to the forest, Alex and Martin gazed at the emptiness in the air with no idea what to do next.

Seven

The monster looked at the five dangling, and then everyone watched them fall to the ground, followed by the camcorder. The camcorder fell a few feet away from Marco and shattered into pieces.

"Nooo!" said Marco in pain and surprise.

The monster was about to place its giant foot on the newcomers lying on the ground when a portal opened up all of a sudden. The monster placed its foot on the portal and got sucked into it and was gone. All looked at the newcomers. Marco, Sasha, Matt, and Rachel looked at Jane, and Marco asked, "Where did you send it . . . our universe?"

"Don't know. We need to go back and see," said Jane. Another portal opened up, and the five dived in. The portal closed and opened up in New Winterwood Park, which they had left a few minutes earlier.

Everything was calm and quiet. Alex and Martin were surprised when a portal opened up a few feet away, and out flew Marco, Matt, Rachel, Sasha, and Jane.

"You lot are safe and back!" said Martin as he and Alex hugged Sasha with joy.

"Where's the monster?" asked Jane.

"What monster? Which monster?" asked Alex.

"There's no monster here, Jane," Martin said.

Jane, Rachel, Matt, and Marco looked at their surroundings. There was peace and quietness all around.

No sign of the monster. Marco told them everything. Alex and Martin listened with amazement.

"We saw our pals, but because of that damn monster," said Jane, "we didn't wait to talk, fearing it came here."

Sasha said, "That means you can open portals to other universes too, not just between ours and theirs."

Just then, Stella, Steve, Andrews, and Maria came running.

The gang got up, looking at their pals from another universe running toward them in confusion.

"How did you go there, and where's the monster? Did you catch it so fast? And are you okay?" asked Andrews, leaning toward Jane, taking her hand.

"The monster went somewhere else," said Marco.

"How did you go there and back, and where is the portal opener?" asked Steve.

Matt pointed to Jane and said, "She is the portal opener."

"*Whaattt!*" said the four new comers in unison and amazement.

Meanwhile, in one of the many universes, the monster appeared in an alien environment, and it was going to attack the minute cities around when a large foot landed on it, crushing it into the ground.

"Silly pests," said a man as big as a mountain to that monster as it was to the people whom it was terrorizing.

The monster got crushed into the snowy ground.

"There are 126 universes. This is stated officially as Realm 115, and ours is Realm 002. And you have made the maximum connection to our universe not just because of love or want but because of your connection with both the universes, your birth," said Maria, looking at the others who were sitting on the cushioned sofa and chairs in Jane's house.

All were back in Jane's house and were discussing about the recent portal openings and Sasha's theory.

Marco looked worried."What's the thing that's bugging you, dear?" asked Sasha.

"Today my bro's gonna kill me," replied Marco.

"Ohh . . . Don't tell him you took that camcorder out," said Martin.

"I can't coz he saw me taking it," said Marco.

"We'll miss you, buddy," said Matt teasingly. "You were a very good friend and a wonderful creator of Hunters."

Rachel held her laughter but broke out laughing when Marco ran after Matt, picking up a vase to hit him.

Steve thought it was best if they get help from Dave as he was more experienced in operating the portals and being a chief too.

All eleven decided to go to Realm 002. Steve, Stella, and Martin stayed behind in case a need for Hunters arose in Realm 115.

"The general is good and clever, so he's the general," said Steve, amused with the appearance of the portal.

He looked at a surprised Matt, flashing his teeth, and said before Matt would say anything, "We had told Dave, our general, to open up a portal after forty-five minutes and send in troops if necessary. Heee."

Matt nodded his head in agreement, and then Alex, Sasha, Maria, Andrews, Marco, Matt, Rachel, and Jane walked into the portal one after another.

In PAC, everyone was armed, and out of the portal came Maria and Andrews, followed by Sasha, Marco, and Alex, then Jane, Rachel, and Matt.

All were thrilled to see the legendary Hunters and Queen Akilo's daughter, Jane.

"Welcome, Great-Aunt," said a red-haired young man to Jane. He was also four years younger to her and seemed to be in his twenties. "I'm Prince Ralph, your great grand nephew, I guess."

They all bowed to Jane to welcome her.

"My, this realm's family knows me," said Jane, amused.

"Yeah, of course, everyone does," said Andrews, "and that too the royal ones, so from 115's lonely resident to 002's royal resident."

Jane looked at Andrews.

"What did I say wrong?" said Andrews and teased her by saying softly, "Your Highness?"

By now they all got up when Dave announced, "We have among us the legendary Hunters and Shen-vom Dynasty's Princess Jane." Everyone clapped.

"Or in fact, the true queen, Queen Jane," said Ralph.

Soon it was stated that portal travel had somehow manipulated Jane's body when she was in her mom's womb as Sasha had theorized, and so she had the power to travel through universes.

Everyone came to a conclusion that if Jane underwent some practice, she could open a portal whenever she wants and to wherever she wants. The visitors decided to return to Realm 115 the next day, and so they went sightseeing and shopping. Rachel, Marco, and Matt wore masks given to them by Dave to cover their faces so as not to attract attention from the public as Marissa, Jordan, and Kyle were famous. Though they had only been in that universe for a short term, they were indeed famous. They became stars by creating Hunters here too and giving knowledge about universal jump. There was a statue of all three at the headquarters as well as one in the centre of the city.

Jane decided to return to Realm 115 after meeting her folks and spending time with them and Andrews and also practicing her skills. Alex decided to stay behind so that Jane would be accompanied by someone from their realm while the others left.

It had been two days since they left when, just outside Jane's house, a portal appeared.

Stella was watching TV, Martin was playing a space race in the computer, and Steve was reading a book. Stella first saw it, and then all three raced to the road. All the vehicles halted. It wasn't a daily thing to see another universal doorway appear one fine morning.

Out stepped Marco, Matt, Rachel, and Sasha.

They looked at each other, and before Martin, Steve, or Stella could ask, Marco said, "Jane is meeting her folks, and Alex is staying behind to give Jane company."

"Company when she's surrounded by her folks?" asked Martin, confused.

"You know, company with someone from her world," said Sasha.

"That's her world too," said Martin, amused.

"Well, Stella and Steve, thanks for keeping watch, but now your world might need you back," said Marco.

Stella and Steve shook hands with the four and walked into the portal, then it closed.

Rachel looked around and saw people looking at them. She lowered her head and said to her friends, "Let's go in and talk."

All walked to the house.

Marco placed the new camcorder on the table.

"Okay," said Martin, "you got one."

"Yeah, gotta replace the one I got destroyed," said Marco, placing a polythene bag containing the earlier camcorder's pieces.

"Well, what's that for?" asked Martin.

"To remind him or so that his bro can perform the last rites to his old camcorder," said Matt, laughing.

Again Matt was chased by Marco, with a stick this time, around the house, and Marco was hitting him on his head.

Jane met her family members, and then she met some mountain tribe folks. From them, she learned to relax her mind, which helped her in summoning more than one portal in one day.

One day while summoning a portal, Jane tried to make it stay open for fifteen minutes. Her skills were improving, and she was able to open a portal to any of the 126 universes scattered across. A small green frog was jumping across the lawn when the portal was summoned. It stood still and croaked and jumped into it after five minutes.

It was a normal day for Flireon. Few elves came to kill him, and they lost. As he was fighting them, a portal opened up. It was there for some twenty minutes, but none came through, nor did anyone go through for some time. Flireon was wondering what it was when he saw a small green frog come through and disappear in the river flowing by.

Flireon flew toward the lake, and it was easy to spot a green frog in the yellow shore with few grasses. Flireon transformed into his human-like form and grabbed the frog. Now Flireon held its head into his mouth and closed it, cutting the frog in two. He began to chew it and thus began to extract its mind. He soon realized that this was a portal and that a beautiful young lady with long black hair, Jane, was the one who summoned it.

"With her, I can conquer everything!" growled Flireon.

One day Jane summoned a portal to a random realm, which happened to be Realm 001 by coincidence. She kept it open as she saw the portal's surrounding scene in her head. *(With her power, she can also see the surroundings as long as the portal stays open.)*

Flireon was flying across when he saw far below a portal appear again, and he sped toward it.

Next was quick as something came out of the portal in a flash. It landed on the lawn, destroying the flowers.

The portal too closed as Jane lost her balance and fell on the ground. Jane turned and saw that it was a huge black dragon like the one she had combated in her other world. Andrews, Stella, Steve, and Maria stood brandishing their swords, ready for its attack.

"Am I the only one here, or is any one of you starting to hate dragons?" said Maria, pointing her sword at Flireon.

"Hello, darling," said Flireon as he transformed to his near-human form. First, he stood twenty feet tall and then decreased to seven feet tall.

Flireon walked toward Jane. Two royal guards tried to stop him, but Flireon caught their hands and threw them past the walls.

Flireon ran at a great speed and was next to Jane. He held her and dragged her easily. Steve and Stella transformed into their giant mercury-coated Hunter forms. Stella kicked Flireon. He let go of Jane's hand as he went crashing to the wall. Flireon again at a great speed came and grabbed Jane. But this time, he breathed a toxic gas onto her face. Before the others could move, he jumped and transformed to his twenty-foot-long self and blocked Stella's oncoming kick. He caught her leg and threw her upward, and Stella somersaulted and fell on the ground with her face down. Then Flireon stamped on her head hard, pushing it into the ground. Cracks were forming on the head due to the pressure. Steve came running at Flireon. Andrews came and held Jane. Suddenly, green smoke came out from her mouth and nose, and it formed Jane's form, but a bit dark-blue-skinned.

"Doppelgänger," said Ralph, stopping in mid run.

Flireon flew near her. The doppelgänger laughed and jumped into the air. She jumped onto his back and opened a portal, and into it they went as Flireon fired a few blasts at the castle and around.

In Realm 001, the portal opened, and out came Flireon and the doppelgänger.

Flireon laughed, transforming into a seven-foot near-human form.

"What," said Ralph, shocked, "just happened?"

Jane said, "A dragon came out of my portal, and it created my duplicate and left in her portal."

"That duplicate is called a doppelgänger in legends, and if you feel pain, it too does too and vice versa. Most of all, it has all your entire knowledge, and you will have hers too from now on as long as you both are alive," said Ralph.

"So what now?" asked Jane in fear.

"Only its creator can destroy it, and till then, you both will see and hear what the other sees and hears," said an old man who worked in the kitchen. He had come out with the others upon hearing the blasts. "Like sharing pains, you two will share visions too, and if anyone else kills it, you too will die, and if you die, it too will die. Lifelines are tied."

Everyone looked at Jane as she looked at the destroyed central fountain, wondering now what was in store for her.

"Mannn!" said Alex in confusion. "This time we're in a mess!"

Jane nodded sadly, agreeing with him, holding on to a pillar to prevent herself from falling as she felt weak.

After transforming, Flireon just stared sharply at the doppelgänger and walked toward it and said, "Whatever you know, think, and see, I'll know," with an evil twinkle in his eyes.

The doppelgänger stood still and said, "Sure, master!"

"Now, let's see what that girl has to offer!" said Flireon, laughing. He sat on a rock and concentrated. The doppelgänger stood on the spot as Flireon placed a palm on her head.

His mind saw Jane talking with Alex and the others present when he had attacked. And then he dwelled deep into her mind and saw his greatest enemies, Dragoon and Shenron, warring against Jordan, Kyle, and Marissa (Marco, Matt, and Rachel)!

After a few minutes of deep probing, he stood up, "Today I have hit a jackpot. I have the news about my enemies. Ha ha ha. Their friendship split apart. Two are dead, and the three will be dead soon. I'll see to it."

Just then, a troop of goblins and men who were his henchmen arrived. As they came, Flireon ordered two goblins and one man to come forward, and when they came, he breathed poisonous gas from his mouth on to them. The two goblins and the man backed away, coughing and holding their throats. Others backed away in fear, not understanding why Flireon was angry at them. And they began to transform into evil, brutish demon-like forms. Their hands transformed into hard stone-like forms, and they had three horns on their heads. Their eyes turned blood-red, and each had a pair of long demonic wings.

"Now, gotta make Jordan, Kyle, and Marissa pay their old debts," growled Flireon.

In Realm 002, Jane was beginning to feel even weaker.

"We got a problem," said Jane, falling on a flower bush beside the pillar.

Meanwhile in Realm 001, Flireon looked at a pit covered with thick red blood. And then out of it rose Jane covered in blood all over. She now had the same skin tone as the original Jane. The dragon breathed fire on her, and her plain, sleeveless white dress soaked in blood transformed to a black full-sleeved tights.

Many goblins, elves, and men lay dead on the ground.

Jane opened a portal, and she and Flireon's soldiers marched in.

She smiled as she knew that the real Jane had fallen unconscious, then Flireon said, "This can help you for a while," breathing a blue flame on her before she led the army. "You may feel dizzy for a while, but go and do what is needed to be done."

It was night in Realm 115, and the Hunters were busy fighting a demonic saber-toothed lion when suddenly the portal appeared.

"Looks like Jane is here," said Martin happily as they saw her stepping out from the flickering portal light.

But when they saw a horde of soldiers accompanying her, the happiness on seeing their friend got swept away. On seeing the hordes, even the saber-toothed lion stopped attacking.

"She seems to have brought some friends too," said Matt, confused.

"I say, that's not her, you stupid. Look at her," Rachel said.

"Kill them," shouted Jane as a war cry.

All ran forward to attack the Hunters.

Martin and Sasha did a few strokes in the air with their swords and released furious, strong, howling fiery winds. Marco knew something was wrong, and so he started Jane's car, which they were using, and told all of them to get in and then rode off.

The three winged henchmen rose to the air and flew after them while the others ran after them. The saber-toothed cat also ran off elsewhere.

"Hey," said Matt, "can't we use a wind spell and get them all drenched with that liquid and capture them? Why don't we unleash the fiery blade winds mixed with the potion and hit them?"

"Hmm . . . It just slipped off our minds. Good and timely thinking, bud," said Marco, and he stopped the car and came out. He opened the flask in which he stored the liquid and threw it in the air while Sasha, Martin, Matt, and Rachel stepped out. Rachel placed an open book and poured a small quantity of the potion she had in a small test tube in her pocket, saying, "Sometimes its uses come unexpectedly," and winked, and all five together unleashed the blade winds. The potion got flown at the arriving hordes. Most got drenched in it and were sucked up into the book. The demonic human flying toward them stood behind a tree to be shielded from the blade winds and watched his two fellow goblin counterparts get sucked into the book with many others. Seeing her attacks failing, Jane summoned a portal a few feet away to Realm 001 and ran into it. The winged demonic human saw her do it, and he stepped out from behind the tree and flew toward the portal at a great speed.

He caught hold of Jane. The demonic human and Jane were cut by the blade winds. Liquid were splashed on them both, but only the demonic human felt the pull. Jane got a long deep cut on her wrist up to her elbow on her right arm. The portal was near. The pull into that book was strong, but then demonic human fired a beam from his hand toward a car nearby. The car blasted to pieces, and the force pushed them toward the portal. Luckily for them, they fell into it, and Jane closed it.

Just then, Jane in Realm 002 came to her senses as Andrews splashed water on her face. She suddenly cried out in pain, holding her right arm, and they all watched a long cut being formed on her right arm. Blood dropped on the floor.

"Your counterpart is in a fight, it seems," said Ralph as Andrews held her firmly to keep her from falling.

Jane looked at Alex and said, "They are after Marco, Matt, and Rachel."

"What!" said Stella, Steve, Andrews, Maria, and Alex in unison.

As Flireon was thinking about what to do next, suddenly the portal opened, and out flew the demon human and the doppelgänger. Both crashed on the ground.

"They'll pay," said Flireon in rage, breathing fire into the sky as he was surrounded by more demonic goblins and men.

The doppelgänger got up, dusting herself off.

Jane said, looking at them and smiling wickedly, "So you too were busy."

The real Jane summoned a portal in the room itself and along with Andrews, Steve, Stella, Maria, and Alex walked into the portal.

A portal opened up just a few feet away from the Hunters in Realm 115.

Matt opened the book and said, "Looks like they came back to get sucked up."

Others stood fiercely to attack, but this time, out of the portal stepped out Jane in a white sleeveless dress, Alex in a blue outfit, and Maria, Andrews, Steve, and Stella in tight gray outfits.

Sasha spotted the cut, and she hinted to the others by drawing an imaginary line on her hand and looking at her.

All fiercely held their swords, then Jane said, "Marco, this time it's me."

Marco looked at her face, and then lowered his sword.

"What are you doing?" asked Martin.

"This is our Jane, I just feel it," said Marco and walked toward her.

Marco hugged Jane. Sasha followed, and so did the others.

Jane told them everything. Just then, the saber-toothed lion reappeared and pounced to attack. In anger, Jane opened up a portal in front of it as it jumped and had it sent to some unknown realm.

The morning sun rays began to shine.

"Wow," said Matt, "I had never sacrificed my sleep in my life even when the next day I have a hard paper to write until now."

Marco and Rachel laughed.

Marco said, holding his laughter, "We understand you. It happens, don't worry."

Meanwhile, in an unknown universe, the saber-toothed lion stood on a rock and stared at the unfamiliar sky.

Eight

$\mathcal{M}$arco said, "Your doppelgänger sees, hears, and almost thinks the same things no matter if you both are miles apart and similarly bleeds too when one or the other gets a cut." He looked at the cut on Jane's hand.

"Yeah, sort of," said Maria.

"None have ever dealt with a doppelgänger yet," said Steve, "so no one knows how to deal with it."

Ralph said, "There are some books in the library on doppelgängers."

"We have to go there then," said Maria.

"Not all," said Ralph. "What if an attack comes here again? Hunters should be there waiting if an attack comes. So Steve and I will get the books and shall return."

"But why would an attack come here again?" said Matt.

"If I am right, you three have a rough history with Flireon," said Jane.

Marco looked at Jane and said, "Now what?"

"I, Ralph, Stella, Steve, and Andrews will go and see if we could get any info while you guys just hang on till then," said Jane. "And Maria, you stay here."

Stella gave her a band and smiled.

Maria took it and put it on her hand and gave an I-am-ready look.

Jane smiled, opened a portal back to Realm 002, and went in with Ralph, Stella, Andrews, and Steve. Then the portal closed.

Flireon looked at the doppelgänger.

The doppelgänger opened up a portal to Realm 002. Flireon ordered his few demonic troops to go in and kill them. They listened to his orders and rushed in, then the portal closed.

Meanwhile, in the portal between the universes, Jane realized the doppelgänger's plan

"Oh no!" said Jane.

"What now?" asked Andrews and Stella in unison.

"Flireon's demonic hordes are coming to Realm 002 to destroy and kill. We gotta do something and fast," said Jane.

In the castle ground, two portals opened up, and from one came Jane, Stella, Ralph, Andrews, and Steve while from the other came about twenty demonic hordes.

Steve was in Hunter 002 form. He delivered a blow to the demons that flew at him. Jane summoned another portal in front of the army, and they were sucked into it.

Somewhere, the monstrous saber-toothed cat just saw a portal opening up in the sky, and then out of it flew a group of Flireon's demonic hordes. It snarled furiously on seeing them, and they were bewildered to find themselves in a new world with the monstrous snarling saber-toothed cat below.

"What?" said Jane.

"Where did you send them?" asked Andrews.

"Neither to any habited world nor back to their home," said Jane with wicked twinkles in her eyes. "They are with that monstrous sabertooth our friends were fighting earlier."

But as she hasn't recovered well from the earlier attack of Flireon, she fell unconscious.

In Realm 001, Flireon was thinking hard what to do. He decided that he wants to hit hard and better. After a few thoughts, he decided to attack Marco, Matt, and Rachel in surprise, and on seeing the doppelgänger, they won't expect anything amiss. He knew that when the doppelgänger knew about this, the real Jane too would know it too. But now, as both were unconscious, it would be the perfect time.

Flireon breathed the blue flame on her, and the doppelgänger stirred up, but although feeling a bit dizzy, she stood all right.

Flireon looked at her.

"I don't know, but looks like my other self won't interfere soon," said the doppelgänger.

"Yeah," said Flireon. "What can I say? Timing was perfect."

Flireon then shared his thoughts and power with Jane.

The doppelgänger's black suit changed into the white dress the real Jane was wearing, and then she opened up a portal to Realm 115 and walked into it alone.

In Realm 115, in an alley in London, a portal opened up, and out stepped the doppelgänger.

"Well," said the doppelgänger to herself, smiling wickedly as she came across a cemetery and stood before its huge entrance, which was open, "the gates should have been close."

She walked in and kneeled on one knee in front of the grave of some Mr. Symond and touched the ground with her right palm and released a spell into the ground.

Soon, here and there, hands rose from the ground. Some people present ran screaming outside. Tearing the ground, many dead ones rose. Many of the raised dead have parts of their skin falling off.

Mr. Symond's zombie body of a bald middle-aged man rose from the ground, breaking open his grave. The doppelgänger Jane looked at it and said, "Go."

After saying this, the doppelgänger Jane, smiling wickedly, walked toward the street. Soon, everywhere throughout the world, the dead were rising.

Rachel, Matt, and Maria were returning after a walk when, on the way, they saw a speeding car steer out of control and hit a small pile of rocks in the middle of the road. The driver, a young man in his mid twenties, went flying out into the road through the windscreen and hit the pavement hard, and he died on the spot. The passersby ran toward him and saw his lifeless body lying still. Suddenly, the body twitched, and a small sound came from the mouth as the eyes opened. He grabbed the man near to him and bit him on the neck. People began to run helter-skelter. Both became zombies. Both got up and walked slowly after the people, stretching out their hands to catch them.

Rachel, Matt, and Maria kicked the two zombies hard and then took out their swords and slashed them. Both the zombies lay dead.

"What was that?" asked a man with fear, looking from side to side.

"Since when did we have zombies for real?" said another man.

The three Hunters looked at each other.

"Something's amiss," said Maria, and the three Hunters came out of the crowd and ran toward their group very fast as the people stood looking at the dead zombies.

In an African forest, a tribesman was walking in front of a dead lion when all of a sudden it came alive and attacked him.

Everywhere the dead were rising. The doppelgänger Jane had released a spell from Flireon that reanimates the dead when the dead touches the ground.

Flireon, sitting in a castle in his near-human form, knew what havoc the doppelgänger Jane had unleashed on Realm 115 and was laughing.

Many years ago, in Realm 001, Flireon was badly injured and was hiding in a dark cave when one of his men, a thin dark blue-eyed, evil wizard came in.

"Now what, my master?" asked the man.

"Do it," ordered Flireon, "before I die."

The man performed some rituals. Dark electricity flowed across Flireon, and he growled in pain, spitting fire. The dark wizard moved backward a bit in fright on hearing Flireon's growl and lost his balance as he was on the edge and as the ground at the edge gave way.

Flireon transformed into a seven-foot near-human form and descended toward the fallen wizard and said, "I shall raise you from the dead."

The man smiled and said, "It's said that evil plans have a loophole always, and fearing that you will attack me first as that was what you have done to others, I didn't use the full ritual."

"What do you mean you?" said Flireon, biting his tongue in anger.

"The ones you raise are zombies, of course, and they will die, never to rise again if they are killed," said the man, "They are hungry always and follow your orders, but you can't raise the dead. Only someone else can do it for you."

After saying this, the man breathed his last.

Just then, on the edge stood Dragoon and Shenron in their twenty-foot-tall near-human forms. Shenron said, "Evil can never win . . . especially you, Flireon."

Flireon looked up at him in anger and transformed to his black dragon form and came at them as they too transformed into their dragon forms.

125

Nine

PART ONE OF TWO

$\mathcal{S}$oon it was all in the news. A portal opened up just outside Jane's home, and out stepped Jane, Stella, Ralph, Andrews, and Steve.

"Thank God," said Sasha to Jane with Stella, Ralph, Andrews, and Steve. "You guys arrived just in time."

"What happened?" asked Jane surprised.

"The dead are rising," said Alex, "all of a sudden."

"Okayyyy," said Jane.

"It's not a joke," said Martin. "Many are here. The cemetery was evacuated, it seems, on a rather short notice."

"Where are the others?" asked Jane.

Just then Marco, Rachel, Matt, and Andrews arrived. Many zombies were running after them.

"They can run too," said Martin, firing a shot from the gun he was holding.

Matt said, "No idea how it happened, but this sure is a zombie apocalypse."

Meanwhile in Realm 002, Ralph and all surrounded Jane as she lay unconscious.

Just then, a beautiful red-haired girl, Leslie, said to Ralph, "Now is the time."

"Time for what, Princess?" asked Steve.

Leslie was Prince Ralph's wife. She was a clever girl and an excellent archer.

"Time to search for a solution to the doppelgänger coz if she wakes up, whatever she knows, her doppelgänger too will know," Leslie said.

"Yeah," they all replied and scattered to find something in the library as Leslie decided to stay with the unconscious Jane in case she gained consiousness.

After a few minutes, Ralph got the matter they were looking for. He said, "We got a solution, but it's a bit far-fetched."

"What do you mean, Prince?" asked Stella.

"There is a cult in the south, the Raider cult," said Ralph. "It's said that they're capable of cutting one's tie with a doppelgänger by some blood rituals and circles. It's also said that they had freed a few about 5,000 years before."

"That's a lost tribe," said Steve.

Sadly, they returned to the chamber, and Leslie was overjoyed to see her husband and his friends. But the look in their eyes said that they failed to find something useful.

Ralph told everything to Leslie, and at that time, Jane's hands twitched. She was gaining consciousness slowly. Leslie took Ralph to another room and said, "I can't tell this in front of Jane. Do you remember my old neighbors, one Mr. and Mrs. Redkill?"

Ralph nodded positively.

"They're descendants of that cult. What if they know a bit of their ancestor's art?" Leslie said.

Ralph said, "Okay, I'll get them, but in the meantime, you just tell the others I went out to ask for any help from the people I know."

Jane returned to her senses. Leslie came in, and she said Ralph is out to ask help from his medical contacts.

Just then, Jane felt her doppelgänger.

"No, we gotta go," said Jane. "My doppelgänger is with our friends, posing as me, and goblins are posing as the rest of you."

"What!" said the others in unison. "We thought it was she who collapsed and so you too collapsed."

"No, I collapsed as I hadn't recovered from the doppelgänger's creation and I opened the portals one after another. I haven't practiced it for a while. Somehow my copy is in full sense," said Jane.

"But sorry, you can't go till Ralph comes," said Leslie.

"But—" said Jane.

"Look, you can go there, but if as you said she is there with her goblin pals, then you going there will make you look like villains. So it's better you go after Ralph comes back."

Jane too thought the same as she knew her friends will manage till then for sure, and her sudden appearance without a solution might make matters worse.

Jane slashed her sword on a few zombies who came running toward them. She felt the real Jane coming to her senses and was relieved when she decided to stay and come later.

Jane went to the library and searched for something that can help her make the dead return to being dead. She told the others what was happening in the other universe.

In Flireon's universe, a portal opened up far away. Flireon knew Jane's plan but didn't know where the portal might open, and so he looked everywhere. *I should have made her hear me too.* Just then, he had a flashback. It was the scene in which his dark human wizard had said just before he died and before he started his last fight with Dragoon and Shenron, *"It's said that evil plans have a loophole always."*

After twenty minutes, Ralph entered the chamber.

On seeing Ralph, Jane hurried toward him, but Leslie came up behind her and caught her with a chloroform-poured towel on her nose. Jane tried to struggle but went unconscious.

"What have you done?" shouted Andrews.

Ralph stopped him by gesturing with his hand to halt, and then he called out, looking at the door, "Mr. Redkill."

A middle-aged white-haired man in a plain white shirt with three-quartered sleeves entered.

"This is Mr. Redkill," said Ralph, gesturing his free hand toward the man. "He's one of the last members of the Raider cult. And he's here to help Jane."

Andrews backed off.

"We can't let the other Jane know this, so I gave her chloroform," said Leslie, standing beside Andrews after Ralph and Mr. Redkill took Jane and laid her on the bed.

Jane suddenly began to feel dizzy and fell. Matt ran toward her. All the others ran toward Jane, surrounding her. Matt carried her and put her on a sofa in the house, and they continued slashing the zombies when they neared.

Mr. Redkill took out a knife and burned incense in the room, and the room was covered with smoke. He said a few strange words and then cut Jane's palm. Blood flowed. Mr. Redkill took a cloth and drenched it with a purple liquid and pressed it on the wound.

Though she was unconscious, Jane started screaming in pain.

Flireon too felt the pain.

"What the heck's happening?" growled Flireon in anger and pain.

As both Jane's eyes were shut, he couldn't make out what was going on.

The unconscious Jane in Realm 115 screamed as a cut developed on her right palm, and then the unconscious Jane screamed again in pain. Marco and the others wondered what was happening with no idea what to do.

Leslie brought another towel and put it under Jane's nose. Jane's hands twitched, and she rose. Everyone looked at her. She looked at all of them, rubbing her head.

"What happened?" asked Jane.

"Can you feel your doppelgänger?" Ralph asked.

Sasha again splashed cold water on Jane's face, and she came to her senses. She couldn't sense the real Jane, and she felt lost. She stood upright all of a sudden, opened up a black portal, and all of them were sucked in.

Flireon could feel Jane coming and looked to his left to see a portal open up, and the doppelgänger and the Hunters were thrown out.

A few feet away, three nightlings (nightlings had dark-blue skin and the rest of the features of elves) were sitting to ambush when they spotted a sudden appearance of a portal and some people falling out onto the ground from it. On seeing the three faces, they all gasped as before them stood Flireon in his twenty-foot near-human form and on the opposite stood their old defenders—Marissa, Kyle, and Jordan.

PART TWO OF TWO

"I can, but very dimly, and now she got our friends before that other dragon," said Jane.

"What!" exclaimed Stella and Ralph.

Jane opened up another portal to Realm 001, and they walked in, brandishing their swords.

❧

Flireon and the others looked at each other.

"What have you done, Jane?" said Matt. "Where are we?"

"She's not our Jane, but that dragon's. She's the doppelgänger," said Rachel. "She deceived us."

The doppelgänger Jane smiled and said, "That dragon has a name, Master Flireon, or you can call him as your Grim Reaper too." She laughed as the disguised goblins and men morphed back into their original selves when the doppelgänger Jane waved her hand, releasing a violet wind over them.

Maria pressed the bracelet, and soon mercury liquid ejected from it and bonded with Maria, and there stood the Hunter 001 warrior.

Just then, a portal opened up, and out jumped Jane wearing a brown over coat for identifying her and her doppelgänger, with Ralph, Andrews, Stella, and Steve brandishing their swords.

"Now that's our girl," said Marco, smiling on seeing the real Jane.

"So you all are here to die. Lucky thing you came coz you severed your ties, and now I can have you dead without losing my dreams," said Flireon, laughing wickedly, looking at the real Jane.

Maria had too much, and she jumped, did a somersault, and kicked Flireon on the face, sending him crashing.

❧

The three assassin nightlings ran back to the town and shouted about the return of Marissa, Kyle, and Jordan.

"What? Are you telling the truth?" asked a middle-aged man.

"Why should I lie?" said one of the three assassins. "When we saw their friend turn into an enormous fighter machine and kick Flireon, we thought of sharing the good news with you all."

The fight was powerful. Marco and the other Hunters slashed with their swords and killed Flireon's pets when they came to kill them. Jane was fighting her copy.

The real Jane kicked her doppelgänger and sent her crashing.

The real Jane said, smiling cunningly. "Lucky we're no longer tied. Otherwise, I would have felt my own kick." She struck a warrior goblin which came at her.

The doppelgänger Jane furiously stood up on the ground.

Flireon was massive, but Maria and Steve were kicking him into the ground. Flireon got up and transformed to his dragon form. He hit both of them with his tail and sent them crashing.

Flireon rose to the air to fire a massive heat attack, but just when he was about to breathe out strong powerful fire, a rock piece came and hit him on the neck, and he coughed a small heat wave that didn't even go more than a foot.

Suddenly, before he could turn to where the rock came from, a new massive Hunter came up to him. Both Hunter 001 and Hunter 002 have fused into Hunter 003. It was now controlled by Steve and Maria. Brandishing two fiery swords, it grabbed Flireon's neck, landed on the ground, and threw him with a force toward the rocky terrain.

Meantime, the three assassins, along with a group of people, arrived at the forest near the battleground just in time to see Flireon crashing into a projecting rocky terrain.

Jane saw the group hiding behind the trees and watching the fight. Just then, her doppelgänger kicked her, and she lay on the ground. Her doppelgänger placed a foot on her chest and said, "This time, you lose for real against a copy."

Just then, a sunbeam hit the sword of an assassin and hit her eyes. She backed out. Taking the opportunity, Jane rolled and took the sword that was lying on the ground and struck her doppelgänger in the chest.

The doppelgänger was stunned. She walked a bit backward, holding the sword dug into her chest, and fell backward. Just then, Jane stood beside her head and said, "Well, real ones always win over copies sooner or later, sweetheart."

Marco, Rachel, and Matt saw Jane's winning stroke. They cheered as they slashed Flireon's men who came at them.

Flireon felt the doppelgänger die and looked at her fallen body which went up in smoke. He rose to the air and was about to breathe fire when Jane summoned a black portal above him. The force of the portal pulled him, and when half of his body was in it, she closed it, slicing the life out of Flireon.

Meanwhile, Leslie was standing in the garden when a portal appeared in the sky. She was filled with joy, thinking her husband and friends were back, but then she shrieked as she saw the head of Flireon. When half of Flireon's body was through the portal, it closed, slicing Flireon. Flireon screamed and then stopped, and his lifeless part plunged onto the garden fountain, destroying it. All the soldiers who came on hearing Leslie's shriek were stunned as they reached her just in time to see half of Flireon crash onto the fountain.

"Yeahhh," shouted the assassins and the little groups with joy.

They all came and surrounded them.

Then they looked at Marissa, Kyle, and Jordan and said, "Where were you these long centuries?"

All three were speechless, and then Stella and Ralph looked at each other and said, "That's some heck of a story."

Just then, Jane said, "We gotta go, and fast."

"No, do stay, don't go," said a female assassin.

"Oh no! We'll go and come back soon," said Jane, looking at Marco. She held Marco's hand. "Trust me. Hold hands."

Rachel held Marco's hand, Matt held Rachel's and Stella's, Stella held Maria's, Maria held Andrews's hand, and Andrews held Ralph's. And then in front of everyone's eyes, this hand-holding group began to shine, and then they were gone.

"Where did they go?" each of them asked one another.

At a cemetery in London, all eight appeared.

"Wow," said Matt, "you can teleport too. That's superb. Cool."

"Yeah, but this is something I still have to learn well," said Jane, winking and showing her teeth. "I just read it in some book as we were looking for clues to stop the zombie invasion."

The color from Matt's face's drained off on hearing that it had been the first try. Just then, Ralph said, "I too read it, but that takes lot of energy too, and those were for jumping to places, not to a parallel universe or realm."

"So," said Marco, "you got us back foolishly, and now what?"

Jane looked at him and said, "Now we go to the place where she released the power to raise the dead."

"What!" said Matt, "Your doppelgänger raised the dead?"

"What?" said Jane, looking at Matt. "You thought they, the dead, just rose up as they felt bored lying still? But I can't remember exactly where she released the power except that it was in this cemetery. The location is at someone's grave, but I don't know whose. It's there at the tip of my tongue, but I can't get it out."

"There might be about 300 graves here, and we can't try every one fast enough," said Ralph.

Just then Matt's phone rang. He answered it and walked a bit far from the others. After a long talk, he returned back to the group.

"My brother Simon called, checking me up, and oh, he also sends his regards to all," said Matt.

"That's it," said Jane. She kissed Matt on the cheek and said, "Look for a grave of one Mr. Symond."

Matt blushed and joined in the search, and at last, Ralph found it.

Jane drank a potion from a plastic tube she had with her in one of her pockets and uttered some words.

"Well," said Ralph on seeing Marco, Matt, and Rachel wondering what she did, "it's a potion that can give anyone the magical power for a few minutes . . . like two to three minutes."

She kneeled on one knee and raised her arm to the sky and then to the ground and uttered some more alien words. The ground glowed for a second, and then she fell unconscious. Andrews and Sasha held her.

Soon everywhere, the zombies began to fall back to being dead.

Somewhere, a group of small kids were screaming as three zombies of their dead school masters neared them. All the three zombies suddenly made a scream and stumbled lifelessly onto the ground, and the kids looked at each other.

Jane came to her senses after twenty minutes. She opened up a portal, and all went back to Jane's home in New Winterwood.

All were glad to be back.

After a few minutes, through Jane's portal, the Hunters went to Realm 002, and along with Leslie, they went to Realm 001. There they learned that a normal life there could go up to 2,000 years. Marco, Matt, and Rachel decided to spend time with their oldest families.

Epilogue

$\mathcal{I}$n time Matt married Rachel, and they raised two kids of their own—a black-haired and black-eyed girl, Linda, and a brown-haired and brown-eyed boy, Leo. And they adopted two kids—a blond and blue-eyed girl, Sabella, and a white-haired and gray-eyed boy, Shayne. Marco married a girl with long white hair and black eyes, Carol, from his universe while Steve married a blond with black eyes, Cassie, from his universe. Jane married Andrews and was now a well-known universe jumper (UJ). And they had twins—a blond girl with green eyes, Paris, and a blond boy with green eyes, Bruce. Whether they possess any powers, only time could tell; for now, they were just two normal little kids. Stella in time died in a mission, and Maria took over Hunter 001.

The Hunters' looks changed too. They wore black tights, black domino masks over their eyes, and black hoods attached to the tights and over their heads with the Hunter insignia, Hs, altered with a small wine-red 's' on the right corner over the leg of a huge blood-red 'H'.

Somewhere in one of the many universes, two tiny dragons were chasing each other playfully. One was reddish yellow, and the other reddish green. Just then, they spotted a dragon egg. They went near it when it began hatching.

They pulled themselves back as a small black dragon came out of the hatching egg.

Meantime, in some other universe, a young teenage boy of age seven with blue eyes fought with a sword against a rival competitor, a fair bald man of thirty-five, in a sword-fight competition as a teenage long haired blond looked at the match, smiling eyeing her next competitor who could be the boy as he was good.

The End